The Wild Army

Guardians Of The Forest Book 1

What people have said ...

... a gripping story in a magical setting that will appeal to both adult and young readers alike. Well-plotted, written and characterised, this is a book that will grip the reader from the beginning.

... a world of happiness and beauty threatened by the advent of a dominant, opportunistic, foreign invasion. So relevant to today and yet placed deliciously in an imaginary world ... Good and evil lurks around each twist and turn, and the characters live and breathe on every page.

Also by the author

Quests   Guardians Of The Forest Book 2

Gryphon Magic   Guardians Of The Forest Book 3

www.cherylburman.com

First published in the UK in 2020 by Holborn House Ltd

Prologue

Far, far to the north, in the icy winter night, the gryphon circled high above the villages. Her great feathered wings beat the air. Her tawny lion body twisted, the long tail curling and lifting to sweep the stars.

Her eagle head tilted, emerald-green eyes scanning the forest below. She dipped for a closer look, skimming the black ribbon of river which flowed between banks of frosted trees before blending with the vast oceans.

The gryphon rose, heavy, burdened with the weight of the child growing in her belly. She turned to fly along the ridge, one eye on the villages nestled into its shallow slope, the other on the dark waters stretching to the south.

Silvered waves caressed the cliffs. Nothing else stirred.

Weariness settled in her bones. So many years of circling and guarding, the latest in a long line of her kind, set there by the old king. Yet it would not be her destiny to bring the treasure home. Maybe it would be the child's destiny.

She took one last, lingering look at the darkened cottages below, opened her great beak in a high, mournful cry. The long body curved, the tail flicked. She flew higher, silhouetted against the white winter moon.

Her time was done.

Chapter One

The Little Prince

The little prince crowed his victory into the frosty air.

'Bullseye! I win!'

Tristan grinned. It didn't help that his fingers were cold and stiff, archery wasn't his strongest skill.

As his father was quick to point out. Tristan's grin wilted.

'I'm the best archer! It's me, clever Alfred!'

'You are, Alfred. Much better than me.' Tristan's grin returned.

'Tristan!'

Lord Rafe's shout thundered over the archery ground.

Tristan spun towards the palace.

Lord Rafe strode across the snow-sprinkled terrace and down the icy steps. Three nobles flanked him. Their high leather boots crunched on the frozen grass. Their capes flowed behind them like wide-winged birds of prey.

Despite his shout, Lord Rafe didn't look at Tristan. His black gaze was intent on Alfred. Tristan's heart thumped. He pushed Alfred behind him.

'Hey, Tristan, what're you doing?'

'Stay behind me.'

'Why?'

'Because I told you to.'

Lord Rafe and the nobles reached them. A pain grew in Tristan's stomach.

No, not here, not Alfred.

He glanced down. Alfred peered around Tristan's waist, wide-eyed at the stern faces glowering above him.

'Come along, Alfred.' Lord Rafe's lips curled in a rigid smile. 'Time to leave.'

'Leave, Father?' Tristan hated his shaking voice. 'This is Alfred's home. Where's he going?'

Lord Rafe's rigid smile shifted to Tristan. 'To join his parents.'

'Where are my parents going?' Alfred slid from behind Tristan to stare at Lord Rafe.

Tristan winced. Lord Rafe didn't like questions. He pushed Alfred behind him again.

'Where are his parents going, Father?' Tristan's heart thumped harder.

Lord Rafe stopped pretending to smile. He flicked a leather-gloved hand. 'Grieg!'

Lord Grieg hauled Alfred from Tristan's side.

'Hey!' Alfred squeaked.

'No!' Tristan clutched at Alfred's hand but he held tight to his bow. Tristan's hand grabbed at air.

Lord Grieg tugged Alfred out of reach. He dragged him towards the palace. Alfred's short legs stumbled and slipped. His bow dropped to the ground and he cried out at the loss.

'Leave him be!' Tristan ran towards Alfred.

The other nobles grabbed Tristan's arms. His legs scrambled on the slippery grass.

'Let me go! What's happening? You can't do this!'

Lord Rafe, his back to Tristan, watched Lord Grieg tow Alfred across the terrace where the snow gleamed red, lit by the dying winter sun. Alfred's protests rang thinly through the cold.

Tristan strained between the nobles. 'What's happening, Father?'

'Not your business.' Lord Rafe lifted his hand and the nobles let Tristan go.

Tristan lurched. He regained his balance and glared at his father's back. The pain in his stomach worsened. He clenched his icy hands.

'Where are they going, please, Father?'

'Definitely not your business. Think of it like this.' Lord Rafe turned to smirk at Tristan. 'Think of the king and queen enjoying some peace and quiet, a well-deserved rest from the arduous business of ruling.'

The nobles laughed.

From within the palace, a shrill wail carried across the snowy field. A deep voice shouted. A scream was abruptly cut off.

The silence was as cold as the frigid air.

'What have you done?' Tristan choked down the sobs rising in his throat. 'What's happened?'

Lord Rafe's eyes narrowed. 'No time for questions. The wagon's at the gate. Go and wait for me there.' He marched off to the silent palace. 'Now!' he shouted over his shoulder.

The nobles trailed behind Lord Rafe like black bridesmaids.

Chapter Two

Manufactories

The heavy wagon was pulled by twelve strong white horses with golden plumes streaming from their heads. It sped along as smoothly as a ship on a waveless sea. Tristan pressed his forehead to the wagon's icy window. For the hundredth time he saw Alfred stumbling across the frozen terrace. For the hundredth time he heard the chilling, cut-off scream.

His heavy sigh painted a damp circle on the glass. He remembered a day when he and his mother, Lady Julia, had picnicked with Alfred and the queen beneath a chestnut by a bubbling stream. A deep summer green had wrapped the forested hills in a heavy, hot stillness and Tristan and Alfred had played in the stream until they were soaked and had to be led laughing, shoes squelching, to the waiting carriage.

Tristan pressed his forehead harder to the glass. He should have said more. He should have argued more, tried harder. He should have saved Alfred.

How? Would his father have said, 'Of course, Tristan, you're absolutely right. We'll leave this one kingdom alone because you and your mother had a picnic here.'

Tristan squinted under his brows at the landscape rolling past. Not long ago this road was bordered by ancient forest stretching to lofty purple mountains where wolves roamed, men unknown to them.

Today it was a wasteland of broken stumps and burning

brush. A grey pall hung in ragged clumps over the spoiled land, the purple mountains hidden. No birds flew here, no foxes hunted for rabbits.

Just another territory in Lord Rafe's empire.

Would this be the fate of the chestnut tree and the bubbling stream? Tristan's stomach grew queasy.

Behind him, Lord Rafe said, 'You've done well Jonas, while you've been governor here.'

Lord Rafe and Governor Jonas were bent over the table which ran almost the length of the long wagon. They were examining 'output and production reports', or in Tristan's eyes, pieces of paper full of long lists of numbers and incomprehensible charts.

'My Lord Rafe, we work hard for Etting,' Governor Jonas said. 'It's our pleasure to see the duchy grow ever bigger and ever richer.'

Tristan could imagine the ingratiating grin on Governor Jonas' shiny, heavy-jowled face.

'Ever bigger, ever richer,' Lord Rafe said. 'Good, all good. Can't wait to reach this new manufactory, see what's behind these output figures.'

'Yes, my lord.' Governor Jonas' unctuous voice grated on Tristan's ears. 'Manufactories such as this are turning Etting into the biggest, the most important duchy in all the Madach lands.'

Lord Rafe thumped the table. Tristan flinched. 'Yes, Jonas, how right you are. Tristan, do you hear? One day, all Madach will pay homage to us, to the Rafes of Etting.'

Tristan twisted in his seat to see the hint of a smile playing above Lord Rafe's pointy black beard.

Lord Rafe beckoned to Tristan. 'Stop daydreaming,' he said, the hint of a smile replaced by a scowl, 'and come and look at these reports. Time for a real education, not all this stuff about trees you're always reading.'

The tree gazer, Lord Rafe called Tristan.

'Knowing about trees won't help you when it's your turn to rule the biggest duchy in all the Madach lands,' Lord Rafe said.

Tristan loved trees and knew a great deal about them. On the other hand, he simply could not make head nor tail of reports about production and outputs, or why such and such a soldier would make a better army commander than a certain other soldier. Lord Rafe often had cause to rage, 'My only son, and stupid, stupid, stupid,' before turning on his heel and stamping off.

Tristan had no wish to be called stupid. He slipped into a chair at the table and picked up a report which had fewer lines and numbers than others near to hand. He pretended to read it.

'This is good, isn't it, Father?' He tried to sound enthusiastic.

Lord Rafe apparently decided to pretend the enthusiasm was real. His red lips curled upwards. 'I bet you can't wait to see this new manufactory either, can you, eh, Tristan?'

***

A manager in a faded black suit which had once clothed a better fed man, bowed low, welcoming Lord Rafe to this newest of his lordship's ventures. Rows of clerks and secretaries stood between piles of brown, slushy snow to line the path to the mighty timber and iron building.

Tristan couldn't help noticing the frayed cuffs at the ends of otherwise clean and neat sleeves, and the many pairs of damp-stained, down-at-heel shoes. Few of his lordship's subjects wore warm coats to resist the bitter wind gusting across the naked surrounding plain. Tristan shivered, uncomfortably aware of his fur hat sitting snugly on his brown curls and of his long-sleeved velvet tunic, leather leggings and fur-lined cloak. He deliberately didn't pull the cloak closer about his well-covered shoulders.

The clerks and secretaries hung their heads, studying the

brown slush rather than welcoming their overlord.

Tristan followed the manager, Lord Rafe and Governor Jonas along the path to the vast manufactory with its tall, belching chimneys. Flames and smoke filled the space beyond the wide, open doors. There was a racket of screeching machinery and thumping engines. The smell of molten metal and burning charcoal lay heavy on the cold air.

Tristan hesitated. He'd visited Lord Rafe's manufactories before. Inside, he knew, glowing, towering furnaces smelted ore to turn into weapons and armour for Etting's soldiers. Sweating men shovelled chunks of charcoal into the furnaces, stoking the heat, their bare arms scorched, their eyes dead.

'Rafe! You, Rafe!'

The anguished cry tore at Tristan's heart. The three men ahead stumbled into each other as a bedraggled woman with wild hair and skinny arms threw herself at their feet.

'See what you have done!'

The woman pushed a bundle of rags into Lord Rafe's hands. He took it, staring into the distress of her swollen face. The manager rushed forward to tug at the woman's thin clothing, urging her away.

Lord Rafe's soldiers reached their master just as Lord Rafe realised what the bundle was. His face went white, his black eyes widened. He held the bundle at arms' length.

Tristan frowned. What was it?

'My babe!' the woman shrieked. 'My babe!'

The manager kept tugging. The woman resisted, keening in a high-pitched whine which sent shivers rippling down Tristan's back despite his fur-lined cloak.

'You, Rafe,' the woman sobbed, hands stretched forward, 'this is your doing. See what you have done.'

Lord Rafe gaped at the bundle in his hands. Tristan saw Governor Jonas scurry into the building like a rat into a hole. A soldier wrenched the bundle from Lord Rafe and thrust it at the woman. She clutched it to her scrawny chest as the manager dragged her off the path. Another soldier ushered Lord Rafe along, shielding him from the woman, leading him after Governor Jonas into the smoke and flames of the manufactory.

Tristan's legs were lead. Except for the wracking sobs of the bereaved mother, now a heap at the manager's feet, the silence was as deep as that which followed the shouting at the little prince's palace.

The manager touched the woman on her threadbare back.

'Go home and bury him, Ida,' he said gently. He summoned two clerks. 'Take care of her.'

He straightened up, tugged at his over-large suit coat, and marched towards the manufactory.

Tristan waited. No one spoke to him.

He hoped they didn't realise he was Lord Rafe's son.

He hoped – knowing it was a futile hope – that the image of the pitiful bundle of rags and the sobbing mother wouldn't forever fill his nights.

Chapter Three

The Tower

Lord Rafe rested his gloved hands on the tower's cold parapet. To his left, the sun protested its bedtime in a blazing temper of gold and red, but Lord Rafe had no interest in the sun's glorious tantrum. He gazed northwards, past a line of gaunt, grey trees on the tops of the nearby hills.

He sighed, and slowly turned to take in the views to the east, south and west. With his back to the northern trees, Lord Rafe's full lips twitched in a self-satisfied smile. All he could see before him, all he had visited these past weeks, and much more, belonged to him, Rafe of Etting.

Lord Rafe stroked his short black beard. It hadn't always been the case. Not long ago, his duchy wasn't big enough to notice.

'Small but perfect,' he said to the evening air. His breath misted before his face.

It's what Julia used to say. Lord Rafe squirmed, remembering how he would tease his beautiful, pale wife. 'Like you, my dear,' he would tell her and they would laugh.

Julia's laughter was gone now. Those stupid doctors who couldn't save her, or the child. Lord Rafe had buried his own laughter with his wife and his daughter and had set his energies to turning Etting into a perfect, but very big duchy.

He'd had to build his army along the way, starting with mercenaries, then adding the conscripts – all those farm boys and apprentices excited about playing soldiers, for real, with real weapons.

Lord Rafe snorted. He well knew there wasn't much excitement in the conscripts these days. Mostly because they came from Etting's former neighbours, countries swept up by the new army to build the big empire.

Not that the empire was complete yet.

Lord Rafe twisted about and stared northwards again, to where the line of gaunt trees had sunk into the night.

He comforted himself with Jonas' claim that Etting was now the biggest of all the Madach duchies. And in safe hands too, governed by noble friends like Jonas and Lord Grieg, loyal to Etting, loyal to him.

Jonas. Lord Rafe's thoughts flew to the shameful scene outside the manufactory, the wailing woman, the bundle thrust into his unsuspecting hands. How was it his fault the baby died? Lord Rafe could have told the woman babies do die. He knew.

It was a pity Tristan had witnessed the whole thing. Lord Rafe had felt Tristan's sidelong glances during the rest of the tour of the empire, as if Tristan suspected it was, somehow, truly Lord Rafe's fault about the baby. As if Tristan harboured secret worries about how the people of the growing empire were treated.

Tristan hadn't mentioned it though.

Lord Rafe humphed. 'The people are fine,' he said out loud. 'Tristan needs to grow up.'

Lord Rafe had been too soft on Tristan. If the boy was going to inherit the biggest duchy in all the Madach lands, he needed to toughen up, and pretty smartly. Lord Rafe had a plan to make this happen. He'd already sent Tristan's tutors away.

'You've had enough education,' he'd said to Tristan when they'd returned from the tour. 'Time for you to learn about the real world.'

Lord Rafe humphed again. What he had in mind would be the making of the boy.

He shivered as the night's chill fingers stroked his bare neck. He shrugged the soft fur of his cloak more closely about his shoulders and turned his back on the view of the tiny dots of light from the cottage windows scattered along the dark valley below. He marched across the roof, ducked his head under the low doorway, and stepped into the well lit stairwell.

Chapter Four

The Northern Expedition

'Tristan, hurry up!'

Lord Rafe tapped his riding crop against his soft leather leggings as if Tristan was a dog to be called to heel.

'Haven't got all day.'

He didn't wait for Tristan. He hurried up the gangplank, the clack-clack of his jewel-studded boots on the ramp's iron bindings adding to the general din.

All along the docks, the shrieks of gulls competed with the shouts of labourers hauling crates and casks and chests from ships to the wharf and the wharf to ships. Wagon drivers stood beside their patient horses, yelling out prices or urging the labourers to hurry, they could fit more journeys in if only the labourers weren't so lazy. In between, a swarm of merchants called to each other, waving their arms, pulling out purses and loudly counting coins while sailors cried instructions to their fellows from high up in the riggings.

Tristan watched a dark gull with a bent red leg plummet to the ground, scoop up a dirty hunk of bread and bear it off, harried by a dozen of its cousins demanding their share of the prize.

He stroked his grey mare's neck. 'Wait here, Molls,' he said and hurried after Lord Rafe onto the ship.

The ship's sails were furled and sailors and labourers bustled about, checking rigging or loading boxes and gear. The gold flag of Etting flew from her mast. A second ship, moored next to this one, also flew the gold flag.

'What by the Beings kept you, boy? No trees here.' Lord Rafe winked at the man standing by his side.

The man's red, cracked lips lifted upwards at Lord Rafe's joke.

'Sorry, Father,' Tristan said. His skin prickled as the weather-beaten man examined him through pale, colourless eyes hidden behind narrowed lids. It was as if constant squinting into the sun meant the man's eyelids no longer remembered how to open properly.

'My son, Tristan,' Lord Rafe said. 'Tristan, Captain Elijah Jarrow, leader of my expedition to the north.'

Captain Jarrow wore his captain's hat low on his deeply tanned forehead. A shamble of dirty, ginger hair escaped here and there from under the hat's salt-stained brim. A matching frizzy, ginger beard sprouted from his chin.

Tristan and Captain Jarrow shook hands. Tristan was embarrassed at how soft his own hand felt in the captain's rough, sweaty grasp.

'Good man, the captain.' Lord Rafe nodded at Captain Jarrow, who gave a self-deprecating grimace. 'Getting our expedition organised. Already got the sailors, now he's hiring the rest – woodsmen, builders, the engineers. Most important, those engineers.'

'Soldiers too, my lord,' Captain Jarrow said.

Lord Rafe regarded Captain Jarrow with pursed lips. 'Captain believes we should send along a handful of soldiers,' he said to Tristan. 'Not necessary, in my view, given where we're going is uninhabited.' He paused, shrugged. 'Yes, s'pose it's a good precaution.' He gave Captain Jarrow a sharp nod. 'So soldiers too. Not too many. All they'll do is eat the supplies and take up valuable cargo space.'

He waved a dismissal and Captain Jarrow bowed, not very

low, and strode across the deck to where a clerk was seated at a small table. A queue of men wanting to join the expedition snaked along the side of the ship up to the table.

'Come on.' Lord Rafe beckoned to Tristan. 'Something to tell you.'

He marched to the bow of the ship, down a short flight of steps and into the ship's chart room. An oak table took up most of the floor space. Great wooden chests filled the rest, many closed, some open to show scores of rolled up parchments.

Lord Rafe went to the table. Tristan joined him, looking at the map which stretched across its width.

Tristan had seen this map before, in Lord Rafe's study. It was a map of Etting's growing territories. The countries to the south, west and east were coloured yellow, to match the gold of Etting's flag. The north was mostly coloured blue, for the oceans, the blue stretching to a sketchy coastline showing the occasional bay and river mouth. Above the coastline, a wide green strip indicated forests. Beyond the green strip, the map was white. 'Unknown and Uninhabited (?)' was scrawled in large letters across the white space.

'North.' Lord Rafe's voice was happy with anticipation. 'North is where the Rafes of Etting go next.'

Of course, Tristan thought. North, across the ocean, was the one point on the compass where the empire had not stretched its lengthening arms.

Lord Rafe stabbed a finger glinting with rings at the green-coloured shores of the northern lands.

'All we know about this,' he said, 'is that this coastline is all forest. Think of all the warships we could build with so much timber.' He gave Tristan a thin smile. 'Think of all the manufactories we could run, day and night, with all that wood to turn into fuel.'

'Yes.' Tristan's slight nod showed obedience. His heart felt reluctance.

Lord Rafe's black eyes lit up in a way they never lit up for Tristan.

'Should be easy,' he said. 'No one lives along those shores or owns them. We can take it all, and then we can find out what's up here, eh?' His finger shifted from the coast to the unknown white lands beyond.

'Do you know for sure, Father?'

'Know what for sure?'

'About no one living there. It's, well ...' Tristan blurted it out, haunted by the dead eyes of the workers in the hot manufactories, the shabby clerks and the wailing mother. 'It seems to me the people in your lands aren't really grateful for being part of your empire.'

Lord Rafe's happy mood, ever unreliable, evaporated. His face darkened. 'What do you mean?'

The softness of his voice sent Tristan's stomach plummeting.

Tristan stumbled on. 'Why, it's ... well ... sometimes ... I've heard them complain and, sometimes, they don't ...' The image of the tiny bundle burned in his head. 'They don't seem glad when you're with them.'

There, he'd said it. He drew in a breath, relieved it was out at last.

Lord Rafe's dark eyes bulged. The veins in his neck pulsed purple on his flushed skin. He thrust his pointy beard into Tristan's face.

'Why am I lumbered with a stupid son like you?' he shouted. 'Why couldn't I have a son to be proud of, a son who appreciates what his father's done for him?'

Tristan's relief died, drowned under the tirade which broke over him like a storm battering a sea wall. He sweated and squirmed, not knowing where to look, while his father ranted about ingratitude and laziness and what evil had he committed to deserve such a son? The whole ship must hear the shouting.

The storm was a long time blowing itself out. At last, Lord Rafe whooshed a big breath. 'It's about time I thought about re-marrying,' he hissed at Tristan. 'Get myself another heir.'

Tristan wasn't troubled by the idea of another heir. He'd welcome it.

'A worthy heir.' Lord Rafe sneered. 'One with a brain in his head.'

It did trouble Tristan, however, that his father considered him brainless.

'Proves my point,' Lord Rafe said. 'What you need, boy, is a chunk of real world experience.'

Lord Rafe had said much the same when he told Tristan he'd sent his tutors away because what Tristan needed now was to learn about the 'real world'. Tristan had worried ever since, assuming the 'real world' meant more production and output reports ... and wailing women hugging tiny bundles of rags.

Lord Rafe glared at his unworthy heir. 'In fact, real world experience is what I wanted to talk to you about.'

He crossed his arms and granted Tristan a joyless smile.

'You can stop worrying about how people feel, at least for the next few months, because'—he uncrossed his arms to poke a finger at Tristan's chest—'you're going on this expedition to the north. You can learn about the real world and how things work around here. Even better, you can pull your weight for a change, make some use of the stuff you know about trees.'

Lord Rafe grinned at Tristan's widened brown eyes.

'And because it's all trees there, no people,' he said with a triumphant lift of an eyebrow, 'you don't have to worry about whether the inhabitants like me or not.'

Tristan had no idea what to say, if he was expected to say anything.

Captain Jarrow strolled into the chart room. He inclined his head to Lord Rafe before turning to Tristan with a look which put Tristan in mind of a ginger wolf eyeing a lamb.

'Welcome aboard, Sir Tristan,' he said.

Chapter Five

Dark Dreams

In the chilly room under the eaves, Callie bolted upright in her bed, fighting for breath. She clutched her head with both hands and pulled at her sweaty, tangled hair.

Across the dark room, Mark grumbled, 'What? Wass going on?' The bed creaked as he shifted. A snuffling snore followed.

In the next bed, Gwen heaved herself half upright before falling back to her pillow, groaning softly.

Had Callie shouted out loud in her dreams? Her breathing calmed, but her heart still pounded. The nightmare images wouldn't fade as a normal dream should do.

She stumbles across felled trunks, trips on piles of smouldering brush, the air hot and ash-laden, choking her.

Callie wrapped her arms around her chest, shivering, remembering.

A deer races by, panic in its liquid eyes. Three young boar trot in crazy circles, snouts lifted to the air. 'Mother, mother!' they call. Their distress sears her mind.

Callie closed her eyes tight shut. 'No, not the animals, not the trees.'

Birds struggle to rise above the burning air, their wings scorched, their songs turned to screeches. A buzzard swoops down, up, down into the greyness. She doesn't see it rise.

'Callie, are you all right?' Lucy gently shook Callie's shoulders. 'Are you awake?'

The far-off cry of the beast which haunted the Forest in the frozen nights rang out above the village. Callie's eyes opened into the moonlit room. She fell against her oldest sister, trembling.

Lucy hugged her. 'Nightmares?'

Callie's eyes fluttered. The nightmare faded, leaving horror in its wake.

It wasn't just the animals and the trees. Something else gnawed at her.

Lucy crawled under the bedclothes. She drew Callie down beside her, shushing her with soothing words. 'Go back to sleep, little sister. I'm right here. Everything's fine.' She threw a protective arm over Callie and snuggled into the blankets.

Callie didn't dare close her eyes.

***

The sun struggled through the tiny window. It had enough strength to pick out the gleaming plates ranged by size along the dresser, although not enough to brighten the shadows which hung deep in the corners of the room.

Callie sat at the kitchen table. Gwen and Lucy sat opposite, reaching their hands to Callie across the knotted wood.

She runs, gasping, towards the Danae.

'Run!' she calls to them, 'Run!'

Callie's mind swum.

They don't run. Her heart hammers in her chest. Her people are trussed like lambs, wrists and ankles tied.

Callie tightened her hold on Gwen's and Lucy's fingers. She gulped away the dream taste of ash and smoke.

'Is it because of Da?' Lucy's usually laughing light blue eyes were dark with worry. 'Are the nightmares about Da?'

Callie glanced at the big chair standing empty by the stove.

After Da didn't come home that day last summer, their mother, Meg, plumped the cushions, polished the arms and legs, and gave everyone to understand the chair would stay as it was, empty.

'I miss Da, of course I do.'

Every day when she came home from school, she expected to see her father in the chair, smelling of fish guts and salt, grateful to be dry and warm by the fire. Every day, the loss was new and raw. Tears welled. Callie sniffed.

'But it's not about Da.'

'What is it about?' The tiny crease which lived below Gwen's short straight fringe – the colour of acorns – had deepened.

Lucy is there, golden hair smut-blackened, creamy skin reddened in the heat. Beside Lucy, Gwen cries out, 'Callie, help us.' She stretches out bound hands and Callie tries to call, 'I'm here, I'll free you.'

Ash stops her mouth.

The nightmare pierced Callie's mind like an arrow. She squeezed her eyes shut. 'No, no.'

'Callie?' Gwen's voice came from a distance. 'Callie, are you ill?'

'No, not ill.' Callie opened her eyes.

Gwen started back as if burned by their green intensity.

'It's the people.' Callie blinked and shook her head. 'And the Forest and the animals. Awful things are going to happen. Terrible, terrible things.'

Practical Gwen tried to reassure her. 'Nightmares and dreams, Callie.'

Callie ran a hand through her already mussed black curls. 'It's more than dreams. I don't know how, or what, or why.' She crossed her arms and scowled at Gwen and Lucy as if they were the cause of her nightmares. 'All I know is that whatever it is, *we* must stop it. Us. It's up to us.'

'Us?' Lucy smiled. 'What can we do, when we don't know what it is?'

Callie ignored her. 'We have to tell Tomas and the Elders. We have to tell everyone, do something.'

'Poor Callie, to have such nightmares,' Lucy said.

'We can't worry people over a nightmare.' Gwen reached across to pat Callie's arm, her soft brown eyes anxious. 'Especially not Ma, not this soon after Da.'

'No, no,' Lucy said. 'You can't bother Ma about this, please Callie.'

Callie scraped back her chair and stood up. She slapped her palms on the table and glared from one sister to the other. Her mind hurt from the haunting visions.

'We can't?'

'We can't what?'

The kitchen door opened and Meg pushed her way into the room. She banged the door shut with her hip, cutting off a draught of icy air. Her arms cradled a woven basket filled with winter-stored apples, turnips, potatoes and carrots.

Gwen took the basket, throwing Callie a warning look.

Meg stamped her boots and moved close to the stove. She rubbed her hands. 'Brrr. It's cold out there. Beautiful though, with the frost on the trees.'

She threw off her cloak and, apparently forgetting her earlier question, said, 'Nothing to do?'

Gwen and Lucy scampered like squirrels to their tasks.

Callie sighed, went to the door and stuck her stockinged feet into her boots before picking up a bucket and heading outside. She didn't bother with a cloak. She trudged along the icy path to the water pump with leaden limbs, uncaring of the cold.

Chapter Six

History

Callie knew it wasn't her imagination. At the end of each day, the blackness beyond the schoolroom window was not as solid as the day before. She squirmed on the narrow seat, wanting to hurry nature up and bring the long winter to an end. She hoped the warming sun would chase her dark dreams into some forgotten hole, the same way it would chase away the dark days.

'Care to join us, Callie?' Mr Cotton spoke gently to the top of Callie's head.

The girls at the next desk giggled into their hands. Callie felt her face grow rosy above the collar of her woollen frock.

'Sorry, Mr Cotton.'

Callie was grateful for the teacher's gentleness. She'd often thought of telling Mr Cotton about the nightmares, only if Gwen and Lucy wouldn't listen, why should he?

'And what did the Madach do?' Mr Cotton said to the class. Hands waved.

'Tom?'

'They drove the Danae from The Place Before.'

'Why?' Mr Cotton pointed. 'Suzie?'

'Because they'd filled up their own country.'

'They could have gone on ships, sailed off to other lands like the old Madach did, a long time before,' Tom said.

'Too hard,' Suzie said. 'Our beautiful country was right

there, next to theirs. Much easier for them to take our lands.'

'They wanted our fat sheep and huge cows and the chickens which laid monstrous eggs,' another voice said.

Monstrous ... Callie gripped the hard edge of her desk with both hands. Her head filled with a roaring clatter ...

The monstrous beast marches through the Forest. Veils of grey steam swathe its long neck, thrust forward, a gaping saw-toothed mouth opening and closing, biting the trees, spitting them to the ground ...

'And the strange animals too, the ones which nobody can remember exactly what they were.'

Suzie's cheerful voice banished the monstrous machine. Callie's grip on the desk loosened.

'Which is why we never have anything to do with the Madach anymore,' Tom said.

Mr Cotton looked at Callie. 'Can you tell us what happened, Callie?'

Callie drew a breath and stood. The hissing of the monster was fainter now. She'd be able to speak. She knew this lesson by heart, learned by all Danae at their mothers' knees.

'The Danae were afraid.' Callie's voice was low. 'The Madach drove us out. They said, Go into the Deep Forest, go until you can go no further.'

The students strained to hear.

'We loaded our carts with what we could ...' Callie saw it all – stoves and pots, chickens and ducks, crying children clinging to piles of bedding, bleating goats tethered behind the laden wagons. 'We fled into the Forest, until we came here. Until,' she corrected herself, 'those who survived the journey came here, where the oceans meant we could go no further.'

Callie's breath caught in her throat.

... the Danae, bound and silent at the edge of the Forest, their backs to the ocean. The market sellers calling, 'A fairytale come to life, my lords and ladies ... a fairytale ...'

Callie was blind to the schoolroom. Her cheeks blazed, her

skin beaded with tiny drops of moisture. She pressed a hand to her desk to stop from falling.

Mr Cotton took a step towards her. The students watched, waiting. Callie's sea-green eyes darkened, grew round with horror ...

... the animals flee beside her, their fear sears her mind...

Callie forced her thoughts back to the safe familiarity of the schoolroom. She found the teacher's concerned face and was comforted.

'The Madach drove us out,' she whispered. And, more loudly, 'The big, wicked Madach. They drove us out.'

Chapter Seven

Out Of A Fairytale

Callie took a deep breath of the pungent scent of wild garlic and sighed it out.

'Feel better?' Lucy said.

Callie nodded.

How could she not feel better? Bright fragments of spring sunshine glittered across the vivid green of the wild garlic, noisy birds urged the Forest to waken from its winter's rest and the sky was studded with clouds like sheep in a blue meadow. Callie's dark mood had lifted.

'Thanks, Lucy.' Callie set down her empty basket. 'You're the best of sisters.'

Last night, and the night before, the horrors of Callie's dreams had startled her awake, shaking and sweating in the chill darkness. She had slid into bed beside Lucy, who had put her arm around her and offered comforting murmurs. Callie had stared into the blackness for a long time before dreamless sleep at last overcame her.

Lucy smiled and stooped to gather wild garlic leaves into her own basket. She hummed softly to herself.

Callie bent to help, and her eye was caught by the sight of what appeared to be a badger's sett in a sandy bank the far side of a stand of beech trees. More interesting than picking wild garlic on this bright and lovely day.

'Going to explore,' she said, and wandered away through

the trees.

Lucy didn't look up from her picking.

'Don't get lost!' she called.

***

Poor Callie, Lucy thought, gathering up leaves. Those terrible nightmares.

Lucy had hoped all that was over, that Callie's nightmares had fled along with the haunted cries of the beast which had called across the Forest in the winter nights. They hadn't, and Lucy didn't know what she or anyone could do about it. She hoped this sunny outing into the Forest, with its promise of light and warmth to come, would bring Callie some relief.

'Such a beautiful morning!'

Lucy jumped.

'The sun, the trees, the birds!'

Lucy's eyes widened at this enthusiasm.

The speaker was a young man not much older than herself. There the resemblance ended.

His slight frame and honey-coloured skin told Lucy he wasn't a Danae, and certainly not a poor village one like her. His richly embroidered cloak was held at his throat by a green jewel set in silver. It matched the circlet holding back his long, straight hair, dark and shiny as a raven's wing. He smiled down at Lucy from astride a black horse.

The horse was a most impressive beast, nothing like the sturdy animals which pulled the ploughs in Lucy's village. Its neck arched haughtily in a way which suggested it knew how beautiful it was. Its glossy mane was entwined with green and silver ribbons and its prettily painted hooves danced amid the wild garlic as if it was about to take flight.

'Who are you?' Lucy said. She wished she had the courage to stroke the horse's regal nose. 'Where have you come from?'

'I am Prince Elrane of the House of Wood,' the young man said, 'and I reside in the Citadel of Ilatias.' He smiled more

30

widely, waving his arm to the left. 'Over there.'

Lucy laughed. What nonsense! A prince indeed! 'It's nice to meet you, *Prince* Elrane.'

'What a sparkling laugh!' The rider's enthusiasm directed itself at Lucy. 'Please laugh for me again.'

Laugh for him? Lucy looked towards the beech trees, wondering where Callie was.

'I have to take these home,' she said, lifting the filled basket of leaves. 'My mother will start to worry soon.'

'No! You cannot leave! Tell me your name.'

The wealthy young man sounded petulant. Apparently he wasn't used to not getting what he wanted.

Lucy looked up at him, thinking to ask again who he really was. Instead, she found herself drawn to his eyes. Extraordinary sea-green eyes, with long thick black lashes, and a little too large for his fine-featured face. They were familiar.

Callie.

Callie's eyes were the same depth of ocean green, and, as with the young man, they would sometimes appear a little too large for her round-cheeked face.

Where was Callie?

The young man held Lucy's gaze with those deep green eyes. She felt dizzy. A sudden hint of danger warned, Look away.

She didn't, couldn't.

Lucy opened her mouth to say, 'Oh, my name's ... Callie?' The words didn't come, because it wasn't right.

Callie was her sister. She'd just been thinking about her, hadn't she? A white mist filled Lucy's head. What was her own name?

The dizziness grew stronger. Lucy swayed, feared she might fall. The young man – Lucy remembered his name was Prince Elrane – dropped from his horse to steady her. The dizziness eased, while the mist in her head thickened.

Prince Elrane held Lucy's gaze. 'I ask you please, my lady, laugh for me.'

Laugh? Why was he asking her to laugh?

There was an overpowering smell of wild garlic.

Is that why she felt faint?

Prince Elrane's voice came as a distant, pleasing purr, breaking through the fog in Lucy's head.

'Would you like to see the Citadel, laughing lady? You would make a charming princess, wearing silk and furs and soft linens, and jewels to show your golden-haired beauty to the world. Would you like that, laughing lady?'

The sea-green eyes did not waver.

Anxiety licked at Lucy's stomach. There was a reason why seeing the Citadel wasn't a good idea.

What was the reason?

She couldn't think of anything, couldn't think at all.

Faintly, through the mist, Lucy knew her life was not at all exciting. She absently brushed her hand across the plain grey wool of her skirt, touched the mismatched patch on her jacket and, despite the fog filling her head, felt shamed by her faded, wash-softened blouse. Certainly life so far hadn't included silk and furs and soft linens or jewels.

Yes, Lucy decided, the anxiety flowing away, she would like to see the Citadel. She wanted to be a princess. She wanted to wear silk and furs and soft linens and jewels. She wanted the world to know she was beautiful.

***

Callie had tired of waiting for badgers to appear outside the sett and was meandering back to the patch of wild garlic. She peered up into branches searching out nests and wanting to test how well she knew the names of the different birds. The birds eluded her, despite their constant trilling. There were no nests.

Callie cast about the soft new grass between the trees for

rabbits or baby foxes. The grass was too long for her to see anything which might be playing there. No badgers, no rabbits or foxes. Not even a deer to be seen.

There was something Callie could do, however. She lifted her face to the balmy air and delighted in the light and warmth. She didn't want to go home, not yet. She wanted to stay a while longer in the sunny Forest.

Callie slowly walked between the last of the beech trees, and stopped.

A gorgeously dressed young man was talking to Lucy. An exquisite horse nuzzled the young man's shoulder. Both the young man and the horse would be at home in a fairytale ...

... a fairytale, a fairytale ...

Callie's pulse thudded. She stared. She should run to Lucy, send the young man and his beautiful horse away.

The young man turned slightly to meet Callie's stare. His eyes briefly narrowed. His lips moved as if he was speaking. Callie heard no words sounding across the space between them, but she knew what the young man said.

Forget, little girl, a gentle voice whispered. *Forget. You're not here, can't be seen. Go and play with the badgers and the rabbits and the foxes. Go and play with the wild things. Forget.*

Callie shook her head to clear the white mist gathering inside. The mist dissolved. In its stead Callie sensed her blood tingle, coursing through her whole body with a fizzy sweetness as coolly cleansing as a summer rain shower.

She forgot about the beautiful young man. She forgot about Lucy.

Callie turned around and walked, slowly, dreamlike, back to the sett where she could see the badgers playing on the sandy bank.

***

Prince Elrane sat astride his horse once more. Lucy gazed up at him, his green eyes the only shape to take form in her

33

clouded head.

'Shall we go, laughing lady?'

'Oh yes, let's go.'

Prince Elrane pulled Lucy up behind him and turned the horse west, further into the Deep Forest. They rode away from the patch of wild garlic, Lucy's basket of leaves abandoned on its side.

***

An old bucket filled with tiny, surging shoots held open the cottage's front door. Callie skipped inside.

'Ma, I'm home.'

Ginger Cat stretched in his patch of sunshine on the worn rug, glaring at this interruption to his quiet.

Callie went into the garden.

'Ma?'

The garden was empty save for the chickens scratching at the soft earth. Callie walked around the side of the cottage to the front.

'Callie! Thank the Beings you're home.'

Meg hurried from the next cottage. She was trailed by Mrs Biggs, the owner of the cottage.

'Where's Lucy?' Meg said. 'Did she come back with you?'

Meg's voice was strained. The hem of her long dress was wet and muddied. Her blonde hair, always neatly tied back, hung in lank strips and her pale blue eyes were clouded and red-rimmed.

'Lucy?' Callie said.

A prick of memory stirred inside her, like a butterfly struggling against its cocoon. The cocoon thickened, tightened. The prick of memory died.

'Yes, Lucy! The two of you have been gone hours, I've been searching for you everywhere.'

'I ... I was in the Forest, playing ...'

That was what Callie needed to remember. How she'd

watched for a long time the badgers tumbling over each other, and when they had returned to their burrows, Callie had walked slowly home. All along the way she'd laughed at rabbits jumping and baby foxes wrestling. It was almost as if she could hear them giggling and teasing and calling to each other. She'd gazed for ages at birds building nests, readying homes for new life. It was almost as if she could hear the parents-to-be arguing over which twig or leaf went where.

Callie had forgotten her nightmares, caught up in the joyous life of the Forest.

'I'm sorry, Ma, I didn't realise it had gotten so late.'

'You went this morning with Lucy, to pick wild garlic.' Meg stared at Callie as if Callie had lost her mind.

'We ... umm ...' What was it? A white mist slithered inside Callie's skull. 'She left, before me.'

That was what had happened. Callie was sure.

'She hasn't come back.' Meg plucked at her skirt, her face puckered.

Fear sparked in Callie's chest. And something else. No, it was gone.

'I'll go to Tomas.' Mrs Biggs had waited to hear what Callie had to say. 'He'll know what to do.' She tightened her shawl and scurried along the sloping lane between the white wooden houses to the senior Elder's home.

Meg caught a sob before it escaped. 'I've been all over the Forest, calling and calling. I couldn't find either of you.'

Callie led Meg inside to sit on a kitchen chair. She knelt in front of her. 'Where are Gwen and Mark?'

'I sent them to look, to the places Lucy goes for wild garlic.'

Meg rose from the chair. 'I have to go too. Now you're home, I have to go too.'

'I'll come with you.' Callie jumped up, took Meg's hand.

'No, Meg, no Callie, you both stay here in case Lucy comes back. We'll go.'

The village's senior Elder, Tomas, stood in the doorway, deep brown eyebrows furrowed over piercing, midnight blue eyes. He held a thick stick in one calloused hand. The other hand waved behind him at the villagers gathered in the lane.

Callie's spark of fear dimmed. Tomas would know what to do. He always did.

Meg sat down heavily, keeping hold of Callie's hand. 'Yes, Tomas, you're right. We should stay here, in case, in case ...'

'You mustn't worry. Likely she's had a fall, hurt her ankle and can't walk, or got herself lost. Probably on her way back with Gwen and Mark as we speak.'

'Lost? Lucy? She's walked this Forest her whole life, and she's nearly a grown woman. She's not lost.' Meg's eyes brimmed. 'She must be hurt, poor thing.'

Callie squeezed her mother's hand.

'We'll find her, don't you worry.' Tomas nodded and turned back into the lane.

Callie heard him instructing the searchers, heard the men's responses. The sound of their boots faded along the stony path.

Silence fell in the cottage. Callie curled at Meg's feet, reliving the terrible day when Da didn't come home. She offered up a prayer to the Beings for Lucy's safe return.

Chapter Eight

The View From The Oak

If Lucy didn't come back, what would Callie do?

Last night Mark had been stirred from sleep by Callie calling out in the blackness, fearful of whatever horrors stalked her dreams. It was the same as before, in the winter, when the beast which haunted the Forest had cried out in the night. Mark had hoped all that was over. The beast had quietened, yet he was still being woken by Callie stumbling across the dark room to creep into Lucy's empty bed.

He nestled against the trunk, high in the ancient oak. He hadn't been able to stay in the cottage any longer. For days, the kitchen had overflowed with women comforting his mother while she waited, her face strained, sitting straightbacked in her chair, desperate for news of Lucy.

All the searchers had found was Lucy's basket, filled with wilted wild garlic leaves, abandoned on its side. And hoof prints which went west as far as a grassy area between the trees. There the prints stopped and no amount of hunting could pick them up again.

The tree in which Mark had taken refuge rose tall on the ridge which sheltered the two Danae villages from the oceans stretching forever southwards. From here Mark could see down through the Forest to the sea. The slope of trees and lush undergrowth was a place rarely frequented by the Danae. Impossible to farm, leading nowhere, and with plenty of

Forest on their own side of the ridge, there was no reason to go there. Some maintained it was also a small defiance of the Madach order to flee eastwards until they could go no further.

'Hi, Mark! I know you're up there. Can see your red hair all the way from the village.'

Mark started, grabbing a branch at the sudden shout. He peered down at his friend Jethro.

'Gwen sent me. It's time for supper,' Jethro said.

'All right, no need to frighten me to death, I'm coming.'

Mark heaved himself away from the trunk, wriggling his bare foot in search of a sturdy bough. He stopped. Something in the far distance had caught his eye.

There.

A ship. A dark dot on a patch of ocean between the trees.

A Madach ship?

He shaded his eyes to see better, one skinny leg hanging loose, a bony ankle showing white below crumpled trousers.

The Danae had few visitors to their home at the edge of the Forest, and, forever mindful of how the Madach had driven them from their lands before, they made sure the visitors never saw them. When the Madach did come, they didn't stay long. They would replenish their water from the Forest streams or fell a tree for repairs. They might hunt a deer to re-stock their larder. And they would leave, forever unaware of the Danae's watchful eyes.

On occasion, the Madach might wonder where they'd left the axe they'd used to fell the tree or why a water butt was found tipped over in the morning. The Danae Elders frowned on these risky adventures by foolhardy youngsters, but the perpetrators never grew tired of boasting of them in the school yard or, in later years, the village inn.

'Jethro! There's a Madach ship coming in!'

'A ship? Are you sure?'

'Yes, I'm sure. It's coming in fast. Go and tell your village,

I'll tell mine. And don't forget about putting out the fires. We don't want whoever it is to know we're here.'

In his hurry to warn the villagers, Mark scrambled from the oak too fast. He missed snagging his shirt on a protruding twiggy stem by swinging out at the last moment, except, 'Ouch.' He twisted his ankle as he landed.

He limped home, trying to hurry, calling out to people as he went, 'Madach ship at sea! Madach ship at sea!'

The villagers tending their gardens or going about their errands, heard his call and passed on the news in their turn. Most hurried inside to tend to their fires. Others made their way to the Viewing Point for a glimpse of the incoming ship.

***

Callie sat at the kitchen table watching Gwen, hands and apron white with flour, make bread. With each slap of the dough, tiny grains of wheat bounced into the air and fell back onto the floury wood.

Meg, upright in her chair, hands folded in the lap of her dark skirt, never took her eyes off the open cottage door in case she might miss a message from the searchers. The women keeping her company murmured among themselves.

Callie blew out a long, impatient breath and Gwen gave her a small sympathetic smile.

They all heard the call. 'Madach ship at sea!'

Meg's head lifted at the sound of Mark's voice. She blinked at her visitors, as if surprised by their presence.

'Go,' she said to them, standing up with sudden energy to shoo them out like a brood of hens. 'Go and see to your fires.'

Gwen turned to the stove, wiping her hands on a towel and grumbling about wasted dough.

A searcher came in and made his way through the departing neighbours. Meg ran to meet him.

***

Callie had no idea any of this was happening.

At Mark's call, she had gasped and sprung from her chair. Now she stood, arms rigid at her sides.

The hissing monster of her nightmare loomed above her, there in the sunlit kitchen.

... a scarred desolation of torn stumps scattered in the monster's wake ... the fear of the animals searing her mind ... panicked birds screeching overhead ...

She must hide, hide away from the hissing monster.

... the Danae, standing silent at the edge of the Forest, hands bound. The market sellers calling, 'A fairytale come to life, my lords and ladies ... a fairytale ...'

She must hide, hide away from the calls of the market sellers.

***

In the flurry of the women leaving and Mark shouting about the Madach no one noticed Callie's silent distress.

Gwen damped the fire and turned around.

'Callie, where are you?'

Meg was by the door, listening to the searcher. A glance told Gwen the news was not good.

'Callie?' Gwen checked the corners as if Callie might have squashed herself into the shadows and become invisible.

She was about to look in the other room when she heard a torn sob from under the table. Gwen bent to find Callie clutching Ginger Cat to her chest. Streaming tears wet Callie's red and swollen face and soaked into the collar of her frock.

Gwen crouched on the floor.

'What's wrong? Is it because of Lucy? Poor Callie, come out of there and let me give you a hug.'

Callie wouldn't come out. She turned blank, dark eyes to Gwen. 'The Forest, the Forest!'

'The Forest? What do you mean?'

Gwen stretched for Callie, hushing her.

Callie rocked back and forth, arms wrapped around the

struggling cat. 'The animals, the birds, no, not the Forest!'

Meg came running, wringing her hands. She squatted on the floor too. 'What's wrong, Callie? What's the matter?'

The nightmares, Gwen remembered. An abrupt panic caused her heart to miss a beat. She climbed under the table too and held Callie until her tears were done.

Meg paced up and down, her own eyes wet.

A dull anxiety picked at Gwen's mind.

***

'There're two ships,' whispered Jethro.

'Why are you whispering?' Mark said. 'They can't hear us from here.'

He realised the crowd of villagers gathered at the Viewing Point was silent and he too was whispering.

Did two ships mean something special?

Chapter Nine

The Madach Stay

'Enough trees for you, Sir Tristan?'

Captain Jarrow appeared at Tristan's side, gesturing with a meaty hand.

'Yes,' Tristan said, 'Enough trees, Captain.'

His eyes travelled up the slope, delighting in the soft new green of beech, towering larch tipped with spiky growth, old oaks still winter-bare and, along the ridge itself, dark conifers whose tall straight trunks towered above their neighbours.

Perfect ships' masts. Tristan's delight soured.

'Think his lordship will be pleased?'

'Definitely.'

'What about the wicked goblins who're supposed to live here, huh?' Captain Jarrow sniggered. 'The ones who spill water butts and steal tools ... and then'–he ducked his head to his shoulders and peered around furtively–'when you search for them, aren't there?'

Tristan recalled the sailors' ghostly stories on the long journey from Etting.

'Oh yes. I can see why people talk about the haunted forest.'

He could easily imagine early mornings beneath the dark forest canopy when the mist-shrouded woods would provide a perfect backdrop for wraithlike visions.

'Over-active imaginations or plain mishaps, Captain.'

'We'll have to keep an eye out, Sir Tristan. Hate to see all those good tools getting lost, 'specially given what your father paid for them.'

Captain Jarrow spotted a worker doing nothing. 'Hey, you over there! D'you think you're on holiday?'

He strutted off to shout more conveniently at other workers. Captain Jarrow, Tristan had learned, did nearly as much shouting as Lord Rafe.

Tristan stood a while in the warming sun watching men unload crates, take out axes, hoes and small scythes and push their way through the undergrowth at the edge of the rocky shoreline. Heavy stakes were being driven into the ground at various marked spots – the beginnings, he knew, of a wharf.

Store sheds would be built on the wharf. It was also where the engineers Lord Rafe considered so crucial to the expedition would build the huge machines waiting in pieces in the holds of the ships.

Tristan sighed and patted his pockets. He had his new leather notebook and pencils. He pushed his way into the bushes to begin his work of surveying the forest.

It was hard work despite the overgrown animal trail he stumbled upon not too far from the shore. He fought his way up the hill, ducking under overhanging bushes and knobbly twigs which clawed at his clothes. He soon grew hot and sticky.

While he struggled, Tristan mulled over what Captain Jarrow had said. Not about the goblins. No. He thought about his father being pleased. Tristan knew this was by no means an easy task. It was much easier to make him shout.

Using a stick to shove aside brambles, Tristan was startled by rustling in a tangled holly close by. He listened for more but there was only silence. Whatever it was, it must have scampered off. Tristan laughed. All the talk about goblins … he'd scared himself.

The overgrown path ended at a fast, shallow stream bordered by a tumble of shiny wet stones. Tristan fell to his knees to scoop up a handful of the clear water. It tasted sweet and slightly earthy. He took his boots off, rolled up the hems of his linen trousers and waded out into the stream to sit on a flattish stone.

The trilling of a bird broke the otherwise sleepy quiet.

The heavy branches of a tall pine shivered, sending green and brown needles swirling into the stream. Tristan strained to see what was there. A red squirrel peeked out at him, chattering loudly, its tail sweeping back and forth in indignation at Tristan's presence.

Must have been a squirrel in the holly, Tristan decided. Not a goblin after all. He laughed at himself. Goblins!

The squirrel dived through the branches into the deeper forest and Tristan's thoughts wandered back to how hard it was to please his father.

Was it true, that Tristan really was brainless? Tristan didn't believe he was. He did know he pitied the people of the conquered lands, forced to work long and hard to create the empire's riches – riches for his father and his noble friends to enjoy.

Tristan's ankles grew numb in the cold water. He waded out of the stream, taking care not to slip on the wet stones.

If his father was right, then here at least, people wouldn't be a problem.

***

Mark grew bored with watching the masts of the ships from the Viewing Point. He ambled home, hoping for lunch.

Gwen was in the garden kneeling beside a wooden tub, her slim, strong arms pounding a sheet with a bar of soap. Through the open window, Mark was surprised to see his mother scrubbing at the cold stove as if she would make it disappear.

'Is Ma better today?'

Gwen's eyes flicked to the window. 'Seems so, though there's still no news.'

She pushed her fringe to the side, leaving a soapy smear like an old man's beard on her thin face. 'Tomas came this morning.' She sighed. 'He told Ma they're going to bring the searchers back. He's afraid they'll stumble across these Madach, or the Madach will stumble across them.'

Gwen leaned wet elbows on the edge of the tub. 'Lucy's out there somewhere, and we can't look for her.'

There were tears in Gwen's eyes. A lump formed in Mark's throat.

'Poor Ma. Poor Lucy,' he said. 'Won't these Madach be gone in a day or two? And the searchers can go back to searching.'

'Let's hope so. And not just because of Lucy. You didn't see how upset Callie was yesterday, when the Madach arrived.' Gwen gave the sheet another pounding. 'I thought it was about Lucy but she was wailing and crying about the Forest and the animals. If those Madach don't leave soon, I don't know what she'll be like.'

Gwen straightened up, wiping her hands on a towel yet to be washed. 'See if you can find her, will you? Make sure she's okay.'

Mark found Callie sitting on the other side of the cottage, back against the white-washed wall, cross-legged, eyes closed. Ginger Cat sprawled, asleep, across her lap.

'Callie, what are you doing?'

Callie's eyes flipped open. Mark had never seen them so green, nor so large. She wasn't looking at him, though. She looked through him in a way which made him want to spin around to catch the evil spirit lurking at his back.

'Bad.' Callie's voice was low, the word drawn out. 'Bad.'

Mark tapped her on the shoulder. 'Come on, up you get. There's nothing to worry about. These Madach'll be gone soon, promise.'

Callie shuddered. Her eyes lightened. 'No, they won't,' she

said in a normal voice.

Ginger Cat woke, arched his back, kneaded Callie's lap with his front paws and settled back.

'They won't Mark, and we have to do something about it, you and me and Gwen. There's things we all have to do.' Callie tumbled Ginger Cat off her lap and stood up to stare into Mark's eyes. 'Important things.'

'Yes, probably,' Mark said, backing off from Callie's stare.

Callie didn't let him go. She grabbed his arm and squeezed hard, forcing him to return her gaze as he wriggled in her grasp. 'Awful things are going to happen,' she said. 'I dream them, every night. It's all going to happen. The trees, the birds, the wild creatures ...'

'Nightmares, Callie, that's all.' Mark's superior tone didn't stop the tingling feeling of a hand running icy fingers down his back.

'... and us, the Danae,' Callie talked over him. 'We're in danger too. I know, I see it.'

Her green stare didn't shift from Mark's freckled face.

He shivered. 'Don't be silly. In any case,' he forced himself to say, scowling, 'we should go in. Ma might have finished scrubbing the stove and there might be lunch.'

'You'll see,' Callie said.

She stalked off, shaking her black curls, mumbling to herself.

Chapter Ten

What The Madach Are Doing

The Madach didn't leave.

The villagers at the lookout wondered at the spirals of white smoke which curled up from the edge of the Forest, near to the shore. Tomas sent spies who reported the Madach had cleared the trees and shrubs near where their ships were anchored. The Elders had no idea what to think when the spies told them the Madach had stripped the felled trees of bark, dug a sawpit and sawn the logs into long planks. They reported a dome of grass and earth which smoked for days. The Elders looked blankly at each other.

The spies had also glimpsed untidy piles of logs littering the edges of roughly made tracks leading up from the shore. The Madach had cleared some patches of Forest. They'd ploughed one into a field, planting potatoes in it.

Tracks? Fields? Dressed timbers? Were the Madach going to build houses? The Elders pulled at their beards and sucked in their teeth. Anxiety thickened in their stomachs.

The villagers complained about the lack of fires and the lack of hot food, and the lack of action by Tomas and the Elders.

When all this was discussed over the family's cold supper, Callie tried to catch Mark's eye.

She'd been right, hadn't she? The Madach weren't leaving.

Mark wouldn't look at her.

***

Callie fretted over the Madach invaders.

Her nightmares had grown worse, as vivid in the balmy spring days as when the beast had cried out in the icy winter nights.

The beast had grown silent. Callie's dark dreams had not.

… fleeing from the hissing monster's ravishing hunger, towards the Danae, standing silent, hands tied, at the edge of the Forest … the market sellers calling, 'A fairytale come to life …'

Most nights Callie woke crying, and Gwen or Meg would comfort her. It was the Madach. Callie knew it was to do with the Madach.

Today Callie couldn't help herself. She sneaked off during a game of hide-and-seek, ran to the top of the ridge, crossed the track linking the two villages and threaded her way down through the Forest. Every step was cautious. She hugged the tree trunks, alert for any sound which shouldn't be there. The shadows were deep, which helped. Even so, her nerves were stretched tight.

Maybe she shouldn't have come.

Callie smelled wild mint and bent to pick a sprig, wanting to enjoy its calming richness. She straightened up.

'Oh!'

A Madach had stepped out in front of her, not more than ten steps away.

Callie's throat went dry.

The Madach was big, taller than Tomas, wider than Matthew, the muscled blacksmith. His broad shoulders filled the space between the trees. He was forced to sidle awkwardly along, ducking under branches, twigs catching at his hair. A small empty cage dangled from each of his huge hands.

Callie tensed. She pressed into a prickly bush, wincing at the sound of a tearing rip in her dress. There was nowhere else to hide. She must crouch against the bush's sharpness and hope the Madach wouldn't see her.

She wanted to close her eyes.

No, she needed to be ready to run.

The Madach drew close. Closer.

Callie quaked as he loomed above her. She waited for him to cry out, drop his cages and grab hold of her.

The Madach tilted his head to one side. He squinted into the gloom, lowering the cages.

Callie stopped breathing.

Please don't see me. Don't see me.

She felt sick.

The Madach looked straight at her, shook his hairy head, lifted the cages and lumbered on. His wide back disappeared into the shadows.

Callie trembled all over. When she tried to stand, her knees buckled. She had to sit on the ground, holding her head in her clammy hands.

Why hadn't he seen her?

Staying here was dangerous. Callie pushed past the prickly bush to crawl further into the trees.

She should go home.

She didn't go home. She waited until her heart stopped thudding and her legs felt stronger.

She had to see what these Madach were doing.

Callie puffed out her chest and crept down the slope. Every crack of a twig underfoot set her pulse racing.

She sniffed. The ashy odour of wood smoke wafted on the breezeless air. She weaved her way further down the hill. The smell grew stronger. She could hear the crackle and spit of fire.

She grew dizzy as the nightmare loomed ... *the air hot and ash-laden, choking her.*

Callie pushed with shaking hands through a clump of bracken, and stumbled at the edge of a scorched swathe of jagged, burning tree stumps and smoking brush. In the middle, a dome of heaped-up grass and earth spewed swirls of white smoke.

Callie stopped, the bracken closing behind her. She gasped at the sight ... *felled trunks, piles of smouldering brush* ...

Not far from the dome-like heap, sweating Madach with soot-smudged faces tossed boughs and bushes onto a fiery pile. Sparks fizzed. Clouds of smoke curled into the air.

A buzzard circled above. It dived abruptly, snatching up a field mouse zigzagging frantically across the bare earth.

Callie ducked back into the bracken, fighting her panic.

Her dreams. The ash, the smoke, the smouldering stumps.

Callie's mind spun.

If the fires and the ash were happening, now, here in the Forest ... she felt dizzy, sick ... what about the hissing monster? Was the hissing monster real too?

And ... Callie's dizziness made her reach for a branch of the nearest tree to stop herself falling ... what about the nightmare visions of the bound Danae, the market sellers calling?

Callie took several deep breaths and leaned against the tree, not loosening her grip on the branch. She was cold, sweaty, like when she had a fever.

A tight anger replaced her panic.

This – whatever this was – couldn't happen. Mark and Gwen ... and Lucy when she was found ... they'd have to believe Callie now, believe her nightmares were much much more than bad dreams. Tomas and the Elders had to know, had to understand that what was happening was the beginning of something worse. Much, much worse. Tomas wouldn't let it happen, wouldn't let it go on once he knew.

Close to where Callie hid, a newly made, rough track wound up from the shore. Two Madach strolled around a bend in the track, straight to where Callie leaned on the tree. One Madach was barrel chested, with a frizzy ginger beard and matching ginger hair rammed under a greasy hat. He was a giant. The other, shorter and tidier, tapped at the stony earth with a stick.

Callie slumped to the base of the tree, drawing up her knees to make herself as small as possible within the bracken. As the Madach grew level with her hiding place, she gave in to the instinct to close her eyes.

Why had she come?

'What's that noise?' the ginger Madach said.

Callie stiffened.

'Some animal I expect, Captain.' The tidier Madach brushed the tips of the bracken with his stick. It clicked against the tree trunk and ruffled Callie's hair.

Don't see me. Don't see me.

Callie silently repeated her desperate plea. She held herself very, very still.

'Hmm.' The ginger Madach lost interest in what might be in the bracken. He strolled on, saying, 'Anyway, as I was asking, I assume it's all coming along well, Master Engineer?'

'Yes, Captain, though it'll be a while before we have enough room, and then we have to make sure it's all level.'

The captain said something back, which Callie didn't hear because the two walked out of earshot.

She waited, slowly easing out her breath.

What else were the Madach doing? What needed 'enough' room?

She crept on all fours to the verge of the new track, smelling the smoke, hearing the spitting flames. Rage roiled through her at the sight and sounds and smells.

And it would get worse.

Would the whole Forest be destroyed?

Callie got to her feet, hugging herself.

The sound of a boot stumbling on a stone made her jump. A Madach voice said, 'Ouch.'

Callie dived back into the bracken.

She wished with all her soul she hadn't left the village.

She peered out to see the Madach kick the stone aside and stride on. This one was much younger than the other Madach and tall, slim. He carried a leather notebook and a pencil.

It seemed the young Madach hadn't seen Callie. He strolled past, head swivelling from side to side as if searching for something. He took no more notice of Callie than if she'd been a chattering squirrel.

Why hadn't he seen her?

Callie's heart thumped hard.

He should have spotted her, standing like a dolt on the new track. It was the same as the Madach with the cages. And the two who had passed by talking about enough room for something.

Was she invisible?

The young Madach wandered in among the trees, leaving behind the burning stumps and the smoking dome. Callie sneaked after him, curious about why he was carrying a notebook.

It was grassy here, brighter, with the trees further apart. The young Madach lost his earlier purposeful stride and ambled along, looking up into the tree canopy and then scribbling in his book. Occasionally he scratched his curly brown hair with his pencil, before nodding and scribbling once more.

Callie kept her distance, hiding behind knotted trunks or spreading ferns. She came close enough, however, to see the Madach smile at a majestic beech. He tenderly stroked the smooth bark of a young birch and bent close to examine an unusual fern, holding the fronds with gentle, soft hands.

Callie's heavy heart lightened. It seemed this young Madach might not be as wicked as his fellows.

Callie had an idea. If she was brave enough. And if the young Madach really was a good Madach. It might work.

This was not a good idea, a voice in her head insisted. Callie squashed the voice.

The grass gave way to small bushes and ferns, the trees grew closer together and the dappled brightness darkened to shade.

The Madach's head went down, picking his way through the grass between the trees.

Callie, her decision firm, pushed through the scrub to get ahead of the Madach. She stopped, her knees wobbly and her breath catching, to watch him approach.

The insistent voice scolded, this was not a good idea.

Callie ignored it. She had to know.

The Madach was very near.

Would he see her?

She could still run and hide. She didn't move, despite the knot strangling her insides.

It seemed the Madach might walk right through her, when he abruptly halted, crouched in front of Callie and frowned into her face.

His eyebrows flew to his hairline and his mouth dropped open.

Chapter Eleven

Tristan's Shock

Eyes tracing a way through the long grass, Tristan considered the riches he'd seen that morning. Massive old oak, ash, beech. All, unfortunately, excellent materials to turn into Lord Rafe's warships and weapons. He scowled, thinking of the clearing and the domed heap where they were burning charcoal that he'd passed moments ago, scarring the forest with charred stumps and grey smoke.

His eyes flicked across a darkness a short way ahead.

A shadow?

No, it was heavier than a shadow. Besides, there was hardly any sun today. Tristan leaned forward to see better.

He was sure there was something there.

The darkness suddenly took shape.

Tristan jumped. The grip on his notebook tightened.

A girl with tangled dark curls stared up at him with eyes the colour of the green waves which washed at the cliffs below the forest. She was short, reaching not much higher than Tristan's waist. Her plain, faded pink dress fell below her knees, revealing sturdy boots poised to run. A sprig of wild mint hung from the pocket of her grass-stained pinafore.

'Where did you come from?' Tristan said.

'Here.' Her voice was soft, like the colour of her skin which reminded Tristan of heavy cream with the merest drop of golden honey.

'You do? The forest?'

No people there ... Tristan heard his father's voice, strong with certainty.

Goblins ... the wicked goblins who're supposed to live here ... Captain Jarrow's furtive glances filled Tristan's head.

'Are you a goblin, a fairy?' Tristan said.

'No, not a fairy.' The green eyes didn't blink.

Before Tristan could ask again, the girl said, 'I've been watching you.'

She'd been spying on him?

'You're a good one,' she said.

A good one? If Tristan was good, would the goblins leave him be?

'I like to think I'm good. What makes you think I am?'

'I just do.'

The girl bit her bottom lip and the sea-green eyes narrowed, as if in sudden doubt about Tristan's goodness.

Then she wasn't there.

Tristan wheeled about. There was no trace of her, except the sprig of mint lying in the dust. He picked it up and drifted back along the path. His mind whirled.

***

Callie hadn't run away.

The voice insisting this was not a good idea had at last triumphed. Right when she was telling the young Madach she believed he was good, her conscience had screamed, Why are you doing this? He mustn't know we're here. You stupid girl!

And right then, the Madach couldn't see her any more.

***

Tristan tried to remember what the girl had said. Something about goblins and fairies? Scraps of images tumbled in his head like pieces of a jigsaw puzzle tossed from their upended box.

He tried to recall what the girl looked like.

Black messy hair. Green eyes. What else?

Was it even a girl?

Perhaps he really had seen one of the naughty goblins said to live in these woods. Were the woods haunted after all? A coldness tickled Tristan's back.

No, it was the shadows, playing tricks.

Tristan picked up his pace, walking quickly back to the new track by the cleared swathe of forest. He knew he had something important to tell Captain Jarrow.

'Mornin', Sir Tristan.' A labouring Madach threw an armful of thin branches onto a fire, sending the flames leaping. He waved at the pungent cloud smudging his view and looked closely at Tristan. 'Are you all right, sir? You've got a funny look, like you've seen one of those ghosts or goblins what's supposed to be here.'

'Not a ghost, a fairy.'

'A fairy?' The worker leaned sideways to peer furtively behind Tristan.

Was it? Tristan mused. 'No, I don't believe it was anything,' he said out loud.

The worker frowned, waiting for more.

'Have to talk to Captain Jarrow, most important,' Tristan said, walking off.

The worker shrugged and returned to the fire. He poked it with a stick to send a shower of sizzling sparks upwards.

What was important? Tristan waggled his head, trying to clear the mist thickening inside. The tumbling shapes had settled, but they were all blank.

He had something to tell Captain Jarrow. What was it? Was it a new type of plant he'd found? He saw the mint in his hand. It was ordinary mint.

Tristan walked on, back to the ship and into his cabin. He had a nagging sense he needed to do something. What?

He gave up, opened his notebook and began writing up the

different trees he had seen during the morning.

After lunch, he returned to his cabin before heading once more into the forest. A sprig of wild mint lay drying out on the floor. He picked it up and tossed it over the side of the ship as he made his way ashore.

Chapter Twelve

A Rescue

Callie puffed out an annoyed breath. She hadn't had a chance to ask the Madach anything.

Why couldn't the Madach see her? This one with the notebook, the one with the cages and the two on the track. All of them had looked straight through her as if she was a bird on a bough.

Except when she wanted one of them to see her.

She grimaced, imagining Mark's chortles if she told him she could be invisible.

Callie watched the young Madach pick up the fallen mint and walk back the way he'd come. She slipped along, following. She listened to the worker piling up the fire ask the Madach, whose name was Sir Tristan, whether he'd seen a ghost. Sir Tristan was very confused about what he'd seen, talking about ghosts and fairies.

Why would he be confused?

Callie took comfort from the young Madach's confusion. He might not tell anyone about people living in the Forest if he was confused.

Guilt doused her like a thunderstorm. She gritted her teeth. What had she done, putting everyone at risk by her foolish behaviour? As if the Madach, nice though he seemed, would have told her what was going on.

Stupid, stupid girl. Of course she wasn't invisible. The

Madach didn't expect anyone to be here so they didn't notice her unless she stood right in front of them.

Angry with herself and fretting about what terrible things would happen now a Madach had seen her, Callie worked her way up through the Forest to the ridge. Invisible or not, she'd lost the will to go all the way to the shore and the ships. It wasn't all about the risk of being seen. The heavy smell of wood smoke, the spitting of the fires and the white-veiled dome of grass and black earth spun like a top through her head. Callie was in no hurry to see those again.

A sick heaviness lay like a rock in the pit of her stomach. She wanted to cry and stamp her foot at the same time. How dare these Madach burn her Forest? How dare her nightmares live?

Threading in and out of the dreadful visions came a noise – a terrible, fearful sobbing noise.

Callie pulled up short. The sobbing wasn't in her head. And it wasn't she who was crying.

Her heart pounded.

Someone was in danger, or in pain.

The sobbing rose, frantic.

It couldn't be a small child, could it?

The thought drove her towards the noise. Scrambling around a young pine, Callie tripped on one of the wooden cages the first Madach had been carrying.

This time the cage wasn't empty. A young rabbit crouched inside.

The desperate sobs of fear came from the rabbit.

Callie's mouth fell open. Rabbits didn't cry.

The rabbit backed into a corner. Its wrenching sobs grew louder.

Don't kill me, a voice wailed.

Callie eyed the surrounding trees. They were set wide apart, the undergrowth sparse. There was no one there.

Was *the rabbit* asking her not to kill it?

Callie bent over the cage.

'It's all right, I'm not going to kill you,' she said softly.

The rabbit, eyes glazed, shrank into the farthest corner. The white fur on its chest pulsed rapidly, in and out.

Callie's hand found the latch. 'Look, I'm freeing you.'

She slowly opened the door. The rabbit's back legs scrabbled on the floor of the cage. It bolted through the gap.

At the edge of a trailing bush, the rabbit jumped about to stare at Callie with brown eyes which filled its whole face. Panting from fright, the rabbit tilted its head to one side. Its pink nose twitched wildly, setting its whiskers quivering. Its ears stood up, straight as soldiers.

You heard me?

Callie blinked. 'I must have. I don't know.'

The rabbit laid back its ears and scuttled into the bush.

The snap of a branch and a grunted curse from somewhere beyond the trailing bush sent Callie flying through the trees. Invisible or not, she had no wish to face any more Madach.

Chapter Thirteen

They Have To Believe Me Now

Callie's fear dissolved in the familiarity of the Forest close by the villages. She rested against a beech, catching her breath before walking, not running, home. She paused next to a group of villagers gathered at the Viewing Point. They gestured at the Forest below, where wispy columns of smoke were barely visible in the dusk.

A woman said to her friend, 'How long can it be before they discover us?'

Her friend sighed. 'Surely we're not going to sit around, waiting? Why can't Tomas and the Elders think of something to do?'

An old man grinned. 'We should sneak down there like we did when we were kids, spill their water butts, steal whatever tools they've left about the place.'

A man in a black hat gave a grim laugh. 'Good idea. I could do with a new shovel.'

Callie expected Meg to scold her for being out all day. Instead, Meg appeared to have assumed Callie was with her friends and the scolding Callie received was for the tear in the back of her pink dress.

So Callie didn't think she needed to tell Meg what had happened in the Forest. Meg hadn't stopped fussing over the decision to call off the search for Lucy, and Callie didn't want to upset her more by admitting she'd talked to one of the big, wicked Madach.

Callie's stomach turned over. Talking to a Madach had not been a good idea.

'I do wish these Madach would leave,' Meg said as the family ate their cold supper. 'Everyone should be out searching for Lucy, not waiting for Madach to finish doing things.' She stabbed at her hard cheese and grated apple with her fork. 'Whatever things they *are* doing.'

'Cutting down trees,' Mark said.

The sights of the day billowed in Callie's mind. Her stomach lurched.

'Whatever for?' Meg said.

Mark shrugged.

Gwen, ever watchful, reached across to pat Callie's arm.

Callie gulped back what she wanted to blurt out, how what was happening in the Forest was far, far worse than cutting down trees ... *the air hot and ash-laden, choking her...* and what would happen if the Madach weren't driven out ... *the bound Danae, their backs to the ocean ...*

Gwen and Lucy's warnings not to worry their mother over dreams and nightmares, sounded in Callie's head. She ate her cheese and apple, not tasting it.

'Whatever they're doing,' Meg said, clattering empty plates loudly enough to send the cat stalking from the kitchen, 'I wish something'd happen to make them go back to wherever it is they've come from.'

Something to make them go back. Before the full horror of Callie's nightmares came to life.

Callie recalled the old man at the Viewing Point and his stolen shovels and spilled water butts. She chewed the hard cheese and thought hard.

Tomorrow, when she told Mark and Gwen all about it, she could also tell them how they might ... maybe, perhaps ... be able to drive the Madach away.

***

The next day, Meg set Callie and Mark to work in the vegetable garden. It was hot and Mark grumbled he'd rather be with his friends and he was wasting this lovely day doing useless work and what was the point of growing vegetables if they couldn't boil water to cook them in?

'That's the least of our problems,' Callie said. She blinked away yesterday's memories of fire and smoke, which stung her even in the day's brightness. 'These Madach have to go, they have to be made to leave, else ...' Callie couldn't go on.

Mark plunged his fork into the crumbly soil and twisted about, his arms on his hips. 'And how are we going to make them leave? Do you have any bright ideas, clever clogs?'

Callie pulled herself out of her nightmares. 'Yes, I do.'

'I bet you do. Did you dream them?'

Callie felt the blood drain from her face.

'Sorry, Calls, it's ... well ... I know it's bad the Madach are here, but it's just a bit of wood they're taking out of our whole Forest. They have to be gone soon.' Mark grinned, as if to show he hadn't meant to hurt her feelings. 'After all, how many logs can they fit into two ships? Not that many.'

'It's worse than a few trees.'

'Worse? How would you know?'

Callie waited for him to scorn her dreams again. He didn't, apparently ashamed at his earlier teasing.

'I went down there. I've seen it,' she said.

Mark blew out a breath. 'How silly are you? What if one of them had seen you? What if I tell Tomas? He'd be furious, lock you up in an attic and throw the key away.'

The guilt which had flooded Callie in the Forest rushed back. Especially as one of them *had* seen her.

She forced the guilt down and braved her brother's anger.

'That's not the point,' she said sharply. 'It's my dreams, my nightmares. The Forest on fire, the animals dying. They're coming true down there, I know they are.'

... the air laden with ash, the fear of the animals, the bound Danae, their backs to the ocean ...

Callie's voice dropped to a whisper. 'There are things we have to do, Mark, you and me, and Gwen ...'

'What things?' Mark shrugged. 'You're upsetting yourself over nothing, and if you go on and on about it, how will Ma feel?'

'Ma?'

'Yes, Ma. She's sad enough about Lucy. You telling her about burning forests and dying animals isn't going to help, is it?'

'Ah.' He was right. Callie wasn't finished however.

'Don't you want to know how we might get them to leave?'

'No.' Mark pulled out his fork and dug into the soil. 'Because nothing's going to happen. They'll leave soon.'

Callie blew out her cheeks and pulled up weeds with vicious tugs.

That night, getting ready for bed, she tried Gwen.

'You did what?'

Gwen's horror plunged Callie into guilt all over again. She stuck out her chin. 'Yes, I did. I had to see for myself, and it's horrible, really horrible, like in my dreams. It'll get worse, much worse. We *have* to do something.'

'Poor Callie.' Gwen's sympathy was worse than her anger at pouring hot coals on Callie's guilt. 'Tomas and the Elders'll take care of it. What can we do? We have to wait and see what happens, wait for Tomas to tell us what to do.'

An emptiness stole into Callie's soul. Tomas. Tomas wouldn't be able to help. The sudden thought made her catch her breath.

'Callie? Are you all right?' Gwen laid a work-roughened hand on Callie's arm. 'You upset yourself too much. Now go to bed and get some sleep. The Madach might be gone in the morning.'

Chapter Fourteen

The Rabbit

More days passed.

Meg's eyes were shadowed with grief over Lucy and her temper short because she couldn't shift Tomas' refusal to send out the searchers. She was forever calling on Gwen, Mark and Callie to do some task or other, changing her mind, scolding them, and succumbing to bouts of weeping.

One day Callie found Meg sitting in Da's chair. She was stroking Lucy's favourite blouse, murmuring, 'Lucy, my Lucy. Lost in the Forest.'

Callie squashed in next to her. She laid her head on Meg's arm.

Lost in the Forest. The tiny prick of something wanting to be remembered tapped faintly at Callie's brain and died again.

What had happened to Lucy? Callie had heard one or two villagers whisper that Lucy must have been stolen away by Madach who came to the Forest on a different ship and landed in a different cove or inlet from the ships moored below the villages. There were enough coves and inlets to hide a dozen ships.

Captured by Madach.

Or someone.

Callie grew cold. She shrunk closer to Meg who squeezed Callie's shoulders.

Was Lucy imprisoned like the rabbit in the cage, except

Lucy didn't have a Callie to rescue her?

The rabbit. Callie was sure the rabbit spoke to her.

The rabbit would need more rescuing, and from a lot worse than a cage. All the rabbits and all the wild creatures needed rescuing from these invading Madach with their axes and fires and ...

... *the hissing monster ... smoke and steam billowing, engulfing the animals running alongside* ...

An idea, or rather the promise of an idea, curled in Callie's head like the surging shoots in the old bucket by the front door.

No, she told herself, it wouldn't work. Rabbits couldn't talk.

***

In the cool morning, the Forest was shadowy beneath the spring leaves. And quiet. A few birds called, many more silenced by the slivers of bark held in their beaks, destined for cosy nests.

Callie started at a ruffling noise nearby and shook her head at the squirrel scrambling up the trunk of the beech beside her.

Callie had escaped the house before her mother could find something for her to do. She was determined to see if her idea might work. It all depended on the rabbit. It all depended on whether Callie had imagined talking to a rabbit.

With no more frights, Callie found the place where she'd set the rabbit free. There were no cages this time, empty or otherwise. The question was, how to find the rabbit itself? Did it often came to this place? Had it been scared off forever by the cage?

Callie rested under an old willow, sheltered by its hanging branches which, nibbled by deer in a clean straight line, hung a short distance above the forest floor. A clear stream burbled nearby between low banks, its sandy bottom strewn with coloured stones. Bluebells stretched from the stream's far bank, a soft purple haze under the trees.

The memory of the scorched field filled Callie's head. She smelled the smoke, heard the spitting of the burning brush, winced at the field mouse's hopeless quest for shelter.

How long would the bluebells be here?

She pushed back her hair, shifted to find a comfortable spot between the knotted roots and thought about the rabbit instead. Strange to be able to hear a rabbit crying.

If she really had.

The sun climbed higher. It was nearing lunch time. Meg would scold her fiercely if she wasn't back soon.

Despite the gloom under the tree, Callie's back grew warm against the willow's rough bark. Apart from a yellow butterfly dipping in and out of a patch of long grass, the Forest was still. In the stillness, her eyelids grew heavy. The nightmare threatened… *the hissing monster … smoke and steam billowing about her, engulfing the animals running alongside, their fear searing her mind …*

Callie rubbed her eyes, forcing the nightmare away. She willed the rabbit to appear.

The rabbit didn't come, and it was time to go home. Callie sighed. She would try later, this afternoon, if she could avoid Meg's tasks.

Then, there it was. Or at least, it was a rabbit and it was watching her. The rabbit's ears were laid back. One back foot thumped the short grass below the willow's branches, as if it was in a temper about something. Its chest throbbed like it had been forced to run too fast.

'Are you the rabbit I think I can hear?' Callie said.

Thump, thump. The rabbit flicked its ears. It might as well have had its arms crossed.

Callie quickly carried on, in case the rabbit disappeared back into the trees. 'You remember the cage I found you in? The cage was put there by a Madach, the people who've come on the ships. They have lots of those cages.'

The rabbit stopped thumping. Callie understood. Other rabbits had not escaped the cages.

In one moment her heart both leaped and fell. She could hear the rabbit's thoughts. She hadn't imagined it. And what sad thoughts they were.

'I'm sorry,' she said.

The rabbit hopped a few steps closer.

Callie didn't move. She spoke quietly.

'The Madach don't know about us Danae in the Forest, yet.' Callie hoped that was still true. 'They'll find out some time, probably soon.' She caught in a shuddery breath. 'Terrible things are going to happen.'

Were already happening. The dark dream clawed at Callie's mind.

She looked into the rabbit's brown eyes. 'Terrible things are happening to the Forest and they'll keep happening, to all of us, you rabbits, the other animals, the birds, us.'

The rabbit tilted its head to one side.

'We don't know how we're going to stop them, and I hoped, umm, I hoped ... there might be something we could do, together with the animals, I mean. Work together, against the Madach.'

The rabbit's ears flicked harder.

Did it understand her?

'If you and the other rabbits, maybe the other animals, can help, can you ask them to come here tomorrow? In the morning, before the sun's too high.'

The rabbit blinked, jumped in the air. Callie watched its white tail bobbing in the bushes.

What would happen now?

Chapter Fifteen

Discovery

That night, Callie took forever to fall asleep, thinking of the rabbit, hoping it had understood her and would be there in the morning with all its rabbit friends and relatives. Hoping between them they could do something, anything, to drive the Madach away.

When she did sleep, her nightmares were waiting for her.

Her heart thuds in her ears, she gasps for air. The hissing monster marches on, ripping the trees from the ground, flinging them to the forest floor. Birds screech above her. Deer and foxes, rabbits and mice flee beside her, their fear screaming through her mind.

Callie tossed, her fingers picking at the mussed sheet. She couldn't wake.

The hissing monster is behind her. Madach loom between her and the cowed Danae. The Madach wave whips, whisper, 'A fairytale. A fairytale. A fairytale.'

The whispers rose to shouts and Callie cried out in her sleep.

She woke to Gwen's soothing murmurs. 'Callie, Callie, wake up, you're having a nightmare.' Gwen gently rocked her. 'Hush, hush, it's all right, everything's all right.'

Callie slept, dreamless.

In the bright morning, Gwen tried to comfort Callie.

'It'll be all right,' she said, brushing Callie's cheek. 'These Madach have to go away soon, or Tomas and the Elders will find a way to force them to leave and you won't have to worry anymore.'

'No.' Callie pressed her lips together. 'No one understands! They aren't going to go away all by themselves. And,' she stared at Gwen, nodding hard, 'there are things we have to do about it. Me, you, Mark.'

Callie didn't want to be comforted by Gwen right now. She wanted to hurry down into the Forest. She wanted to see if the rabbit had come back and if it had brought other creatures with it.

The door flew open. Gwen and Callie jumped at the crash. Ginger Cat, asleep on a chair, started briefly awake.

'Where's Ma?' Mark burst into the kitchen. 'The Madach are on their way. They've found us!'

'Found us? How?' Gwen said.

Mark danced about, full of his dreadful news. 'One of them came up to the ridge chasing a deer and of course he saw the village and everything. Our lookouts couldn't catch him, he was running so fast, helter-skelter down the hill and back to their ships.'

'What happened?' Callie said.

'Stan, the lookout, said two boar raced out to attack the Madach before he could reach the ridge. The Madach took a shot at one with his bow and frightened them off.'

'Oh,' Callie cried. 'The boar? Was the boar hurt?'

'No, no,' Mark said. 'Shame, 'cause we could've had roast boar now we've been discovered and we'll be able to have fires.'

Callie's stomach flipped. She flew from the cottage, hearing Gwen rounding on Mark. 'Why do you say such things in front of Callie?'

The village was in an uproar.

Men and women ran past bearing forks and spades, sharpened sticks and even scythes. Everyone was shouting.

'Over here!'

'Hurry up!'

'Tomas says to go to the track to the ridge.'

Callie ran with them. She reached the edge of the village in time to see a farmer hand his scythe to Tomas.

'You'd better take this, Tomas,' the farmer said. 'You'll be the first to face them.'

Tomas took hold of the scythe with one hand and caught Callie by the shoulder with the other.

'Where are you off to?'

Callie wriggled, worried about the boar and was it hurt, and she must get into the Forest to see the rabbit, because if she didn't see the rabbit, today, Callie's one hope of driving the Madach out was gone.

'The Forest! I have to go into the Forest!'

'Not right now you don't.' Tomas turned Callie about and gently pushed her towards Meg, running down the track calling Callie's name.

'Home we go. Hurry up!' Meg hauled a crying, protesting Callie back to the cottage.

The clanking and clanging of homemade weapons and Tomas shouting orders followed them. The villagers' voices rose in alarm. The Madach must be close. And now the clamour from the villagers was mixed with exclamations from deeper voices.

The Madach were in the village.

Meg pushed Callie into the cottage. Gwen and Mark were in the kitchen, standing very still, listening to the din from the square.

Meg locked the door.

They waited, Callie bitter at having this chance of help snatched from her, just like that.

***

When Captain Jarrow arrived at the place where the deer

71

hunter had spotted the houses, he wasn't surprised to see the crowd of villagers. He was surprised, however, to see the villagers weren't Madach.

The tallest of them might reach to his shoulders. Most would come to his chest. They were more slender than his own people, and while they had normal brown or blonde or red or dark hair like the Madach, their skin was the colour of heavy cream to which a drop of golden honey had been added.

The soldiers and sailors clustered behind Jarrow whispered to each other.

'Who are they?'

'They're not Madach, are they?'

Captain Jarrow pursed his lips as a distant memory flickered in the back of his brain. For now, whatever these people were, they needed to be contained and detained. It was Lord Rafe's standing order that any people they found were labour, workers for his lordship's manufactories, forests and fields.

All this went through Captain Jarrow's mind before he realised the brown-bearded villager at the front of the crowd, a scythe held across his front, was talking to him.

'Madach, hear me,' the brown-bearded one said. 'We are the Danae of the Forest, and we demand to know by what right you have come here, and what your intentions are towards our lands and forests.'

Danae? Jarrow's distant memory rushed to the fore. A child's tale, a myth the old Madach brought with them from their ancient home beyond the western seas.

Was he seeing a fairytale?

Excitement rushed through him.

A fairytale come to life?

'Danae? You say you're Danae?'

'Yes, and proud of it.' The brown-bearded one lifted his chin. 'And you are our long-time enemy who drove us from

The Place Before which was our home. You will not do so a second time.'

The whispering of the sailors and soldiers grew louder.

'They're Danae?'

'Fairy folk come to life?'

The brown-bearded Danae heard the whispers. He frowned.

'We're not fairy folk. We are the Danae and we have lived here ever since we were driven from The Place Before. This is our home, and will stay our home.'

Captain Jarrow grinned. Danae, fairy folk! If it was true – and these people certainly weren't Madach – they were riches themselves, a treasure worth gold and silver. Wealthy lords and ladies would pay highly to have a fairy maid or manservant or a fairy child as a playmate for their spoiled offspring.

These Danae could be worth as much, or more than, the forest itself.

He saw the brown-bearded one narrow his eyes, questioning. Captain Jarrow made a decision.

'We mean you no harm.' He waved to his men to lower their weapons. 'We're surprised to find anyone living here. It was never in the reports. We're delighted to find you. You must be the leader? What's your name?'

'I am named Tomas, senior Elder of the Danae.'

Jarrow heard the relief in the Danae's voice. Taking in the collection of home-made weapons, he suspected this Tomas was happy there would be no fighting. At least, not immediately.

'I am Captain Elijah Jarrow, the leader of this expedition to the forests, on the business of Lord Rafe of Etting.'

Captain Jarrow went on slowly, to make sure the Danae understood. 'These forests are shown on all known maps as uninhabited. Lord Rafe has claimed them, as is his right.'

He omitted to say it was by Lord Rafe's belief in his own right and nobody else's.

The Danae shook their heads in anger and sorrow.

The leader's gaze stayed on Captain Jarrow. 'As you can see, these forests are not uninhabited,' he said. 'They are our home, as I have already made clear.'

Captain Jarrow smiled thinly. 'Yes, yes, I can see. Now we've found you here, it changes things a bit, doesn't it? I'm sure we can come to an arrangement which'll be good for all of us.'

A voice shouted from among the villagers. 'I hope that's the arrangement which sees you all leave as soon as you can get on your ships.'

The Danae muttered their agreement.

The mutterings continued a while before the leader said to Captain Jarrow, 'We'd like to know what you're intending here, what you're building by the water, and how long you plan to stay. When we know all this, perhaps we can come to an arrangement.'

Captain Jarrow was bored. He had no intention of making any arrangements. On the other hand, he didn't want open hostility. He didn't want any of his new Danae cargo damaged.

'Why don't we all go back to our normal business?' he said. 'You and I, Tomas, can meet later in the day and I can explain everything. I'd like to welcome you aboard my ship. We can talk about our future over a good wine and a fillet of tasty venison.'

'Don't go, Tomas,' someone called. 'Make them come here.'

Others noisily agreed with this advice.

'It would be wiser, in the circumstances,' the leader said.

Captain Jarrow held back his scowl and smiled through his ginger beard. 'So be it. I'll be back tomorrow.'

It was only a day. He could use the time to plan how to keep his treasure safe until he could leave with Lord Rafe's timber – and the fairytale slaves.

Chapter Sixteen

What People Thought

A farmer ducked his head through the door of the busy mill, yelled something about Tomas and the square and disappeared.

'Something's happened,' the miller said to his son, Peter. 'Come on.'

Peter and the miller abandoned their work and joined more farmers racing up the track to the village. When they arrived, the Madach leader was explaining about some far-off lord who had claimed the Forest as his own.

Peter frowned, listening to the unhappy murmurings all around him.

While Tomas spoke to the Madach leader, Peter looked over the newcomers. He'd only seen them before from a distance, on the rare occasions they'd come to these shores to fill their water barrels. Up close, he could see the Madach were much bigger than his own people, with thick hands and huge feet. Their skin was burned red or brown from the sun and the wind, and their hair – of different colours, much like the Danae – was mostly worn long and untidy. They were dressed in practical work clothes, as workers, or sailors. A few carried weapons.

Peter worried what that might mean.

There was one who stood out, about Peter's own age. He was tall and slender, clean-shaven, with clear, white skin and short, brown curly hair. Peter wondered who he might be. Certainly no worker or sailor, not in those clothes. Peter admired the fine materials of the young man's trousers and his yellow embroidered shirt, the soft leather of his embossed jerkin and his beautifully worked, although strong, boots.

What really made the young Madach stand out, more than his clothes, was how he never, once, looked at the Danae. He kept his head down, his arms by his side, and was the first to turn to leave when the Madach leader indicated he had nothing else to say.

***

Captain Jarrow and his Madach left the village. The Danae milled about, uncertain what had happened, uncertain how to respond.

'Fires!' the innkeeper said. 'We can light our fires and eat hot food.'

The words galvanised the crowd. They hurried back to their homes, rushing to light their fires. It was a relief to have been discovered after all. Life could resume more or less as before. Tomas would deal with the Madach and some things would change, and most things wouldn't.

'It wasn't too bad, was it?' they said to each other. 'Tomas and the Elders should have made us known long before this.'

'We could've had our fires back days ago.'

They shook their heads and rolled their eyes. What had all the fuss been about?

Tomas was left with Matthew, the blacksmith.

'Like sheep,' Matthew said, watching the departing Danae. 'Anything for an easy life.'

Tomas' mind was on the proposed meeting. 'I'll be interested to hear what this Captain Jarrow has to say. Hopefully, afterwards, we'll have a better idea of what we need to do next.'

***

Meg unlocked the door when normal Danae voices sounded in the lane outside. They were cheerful voices.

'What's happening?' she said to Mr Biggs who was hurrying into his home.

Callie pressed into Meg's side.

'Good news, good news,' Mr Biggs said. 'They might have found us, but they don't wish us any harm. Talking about coming to an arrangement of some sort. The boss, a captain, Jarrow I think he said his name is, is coming back tomorrow to talk to Tomas and the Elders.'

'An arrangement?' Meg said. 'What sort of arrangement?'

Mr Biggs shrugged. 'Who knows? What I do know is that we can have our fires again and Mrs Biggs has promised a hot meal tonight. At last!' He laughed and skipped to his door.

As he got there he turned to say, 'It's strange. They seemed to think we were fairy folk.' He grinned. 'I suppose they know the truth now.'

Callie's legs shook. She fell against Meg. The afternoon darkened. The nightmare filled her mind, shutting out all light … *the market sellers calling, 'A fairytale come to life … a fairytale …'*

'Callie? What's wrong?'

Meg took Callie inside and made her put her head between her knees. She brought Callie water, fussed about, insisted she lie down, it must be all the excitement, it had been too much for her.

On unsteady legs, Callie climbed the stairs to her bed. She slept.

***

Tristan stared through the porthole of his cabin.

Another conquered people.

A flock of seagulls screamed into view, squabbling over kitchen scraps tossed into the water.

Tristan watched the seagulls.

The same as us, he thought, devouring everything thrown

in our way.

It was more than the discovery of the Danae which worried Tristan. It was the nag at the back of his mind that he knew about people living in the forest.

Why did he know people lived in the forest?

He watched the last of the seagulls bear away its scrap trophy in screeching triumph.

Chapter Seventeen

Arrangements

The smell of hot food and wood smoke tickled Callie's nostrils. She lay for a moment in her bed, waiting for the nightmare to leap at her from the dark corners of the attic room. Nothing. And she was hungry.

Meg, Gwen and Mark were at the kitchen table, spooning up steaming vegetable soup and eating warm scones filled with cheese.

'Ah! You're awake,' Gwen said. 'Fetch a bowl and help yourself.'

'We saved you a couple of scones.' Mark grabbed another scone from the plate and pushed the rest towards Callie.

'Are you feeling better?' Meg frowned at Callie.

'Yes, only ...'

'Only what?' Gwen said.

Mark rolled his eyes.

Callie dipped her spoon into the soup, stirred it around. She wasn't as hungry as she thought.

'It's about the fairytale,' she said. 'When Mr Biggs said about fairytales ... it's in my nightmares ... we're tied up, the villagers are tied up ... and there are Madach with whips calling about fairytales.'

Mark pushed his empty bowl away. 'So? We're not a fairytale, are we?'

Gwen crossed her arms on the table and looked at Callie.

'You think there's trouble to come?'

'I hope not,' Meg said, collecting up empty bowls.

'Mr Biggs said this captain was talking about making arrangements, right, Ma?'

'Yes, why?'

Callie stood up to carry her half-eaten soup to the workbench, turned there to watch her family. 'Doesn't that sound like he's not planning on leaving any time soon?'

Meg, Mark and Gwen all frowned at her.

'I think it's going to get much much worse,' Callie said.

There was a heavy silence. Not even Mark pooh-poohed her.

'It does mean Tomas can send the searchers out for Lucy,' Meg said. Her lips trembled.

***

The meeting between Tomas and Captain Jarrow didn't last long. Afterwards, Tomas told the Elders Captain Jarrow had assured him the Danae would not be harmed or driven out.

'There will be some changes, however,' he said, his dark eyes grim, 'which this Jarrow will tell us later.'

In the late afternoon, when the villagers were finishing up their work in the house or the garden or the fields, Madach sailors and soldiers came to the village. They tramped from cottage to cottage, from the inn to the schoolhouse, to the Elders' meeting hall, knocking on doors, telling people they needed to gather in the square. Captain Jarrow and their own senior Elder, Tomas, had something important to say.

Curious, lulled by the belief Tomas was part of this, the villagers gathered.

The Danae from the second village were shepherded along the track and into the square to join their neighbours. Farmers and farmhands, the miller and his son, Matthew the blacksmith, and anyone else working outside the villages, were rounded up and herded into the square too.

Callie, together with Gwen and Mark, trailed behind Meg. Callie watched their neighbours' puzzled, uncertain glances. She saw Matthew question a sailor, frowning and waving his arm in the direction of the square. For answer, Matthew received a push on the back to force him forward.

No one else challenged the Madach.

At last they were all present, milling about, murmuring to each other.

Children cried, for no particular reason.

Captain Jarrow stood in the centre of the square with his chest puffed out. His frizzy ginger beard glinted in the dying sun. His eyes flickered from one side to the other, waiting.

Tomas, next to Captain Jarrow, appeared shrunken from his normal robust self. His head was down. Callie exchanged frowns with Gwen at the sight of Tomas' clenched hands and white knuckles.

Callie's uneasiness grew. The Madach had surrounded the square. She wrapped her arms about her waist, watching, beating back the dark dream ... *the market sellers calling, my lords and ladies ...*

The soldiers drew swords, pointing them at the ground. Other Madach tapped thick sticks against their legs. Mothers hushed their crying children and drew them to their sides.

Callie took hold of Meg's hand. 'What are they going to do?'

Meg squeezed Callie's hand. 'I don't know. We'll have to see, won't we?' Her voice quavered.

Captain Jarrow held his hand up and the villagers quietened.

'Danae,' he said, a black-toothed smile straining out from the beard, 'I'm pleased to tell you I've come to an arrangement with your senior Elder.'

The Danae waited.

Tomas' hands clenched and unclenched.

Captain Jarrow ignored Tomas. 'Our orders from Lord

Rafe,' he said, 'are to fell and carry away the timbers of this forest. They're needed for his manufactories and to build new ships.'

The Danae exchanged puzzled looks. 'What does he mean, take away the timbers of the Forest?'

'All of it?'

'What are manufactories?'

'What have manufactories got to do with trees?'

Captain Jarrow raised his voice above the mutterings. 'None of this need affect the Danae.'

A relieved sigh swept the crowd.

Captain Jarrow's pale eyes flickered towards Tomas. 'I've agreed with Tomas we'll not come near your villages, nor your fields and livestock. When we leave, you'll be able to carry on like we'd never been here.'

Questions clouded the sighs of relief.

'How long do you think they might be here for?'

'If that's all there is to it, why is Tomas unhappy?'

Tomas wasn't invited to speak.

Captain Jarrow kept talking. 'While we're here, there'll be a lot going on in the forest.' The point of a white tongue reached out to briefly touch his top lip. 'For your own safety, therefore, I'm asking you to stay in the villages, for the time being.'

Callie saw startled faces all round, although the farmers and the miller were not so much startled as horrified.

A farmer found his voice. 'How are we supposed to care for our livestock, see to our crops?'

'And what about the mill?' the miller said. 'We don't have stockpiles of flour, we need to keep the mill going.'

Captain Jarrow flapped his hands in a calming gesture.

'Of course you'll be able to work your fields and care for your livestock. Of course you'll be able to work the mill.'

The farmers and the miller nodded, relieved once more.

Captain Jarrow went on, his tone light, 'And, to make sure

the Danae stay safe from the works in the forests, my men will watch over you as you work in the fields, to make sure nobody strays into dangerous areas.'

The farmer who had spoken before said sharply, 'Watch over us? Are we children who need to be kept safe?'

A swell of grumbling arose. The Madach surrounding the square brought their swords and sticks up higher. The Danae hushed.

Captain Jarrow's black smile didn't falter. 'As I said, for your own safety.'

An indignant murmuring rose. It stopped when Tomas lifted his head.

'Danae,' he said.

Callie tugged Meg's hand. 'Tomas is going to say something.'

'I am sorry ...'

'Now then,' Captain Jarrow said. It was a warning, for some reason.

A soldier on the other side of Tomas raised his sword, the tip waving slowly in a line with Tomas' throat.

The crowd gasped.

Tomas flinched his head to one side.

'No talking. That's what you agreed, right?' the soldier said.

'These are my people.' Tomas stood with feet planted wide, as if determined not to move from the square. 'My people, and I must speak with them.'

'Not today,' Captain Jarrow said and walked away, signalling something to the soldier.

Callie's heart thumped.

... *Madach with whips ... the Danae cowering ...*

'Let him speak!' It was Judith, the longest-serving of the Elders. She hurried up to Tomas. With her red hair scraped back from her pale, freckled face, she appeared stern, as if she expected to be obeyed.

The villagers' eyes followed her.

She was close to Tomas when a sailor grabbed her by the waist. The square hummed with shocked ohs and ahs.

Judith flailed her hands. 'What's happening, Tomas?'

Tomas stepped back from the threatening soldier, face ablaze at the sailor's rough treatment of Judith. He tried to reach her, but a second soldier strode up, forced Tomas' arms together, clamped a metal band with a hanging chain around them and used the chain to drag Tomas across the square.

'Keep brave!' Tomas shouted over his shoulder, his legs tripping on the uneven stones.

'Tomas!' Judith cried.

The sailor shoved Judith away. She stumbled, nearly fell at his feet. She looked up at him. 'What's going on?'

The sailor shrugged and walked from the silent square. The other Madach trailed behind.

Left alone at last, the stunned Danae milled about like confused sheep before wandering back to their homes.

Meg's grim eyes rested on her children. 'Come on. Let's go home. I'm afraid Callie may be right, that this is the beginning of some very bad times.'

Chapter Eighteen

Flight

'What are they doing with Tomas? Why couldn't he speak to us?'

Gwen squatted on the floor by the fire in the sitting room staring, for no reason she could clearly say and her mind more full of Tomas than anything else, at the small shelf of books Meg kept dusted by the side of the fireplace.

Mark sat cross-legged next to Gwen, feeding the fire with sticks and gazing dreamily at the shooting sparks.

Callie was curled up in Da's chair, Ginger Cat asleep on her lap. Meg hadn't objected. No matter it was late, and nearly dark, Meg had decided the kitchen needed cleaning. She was busy pulling plates off the dresser and washing them in hot sudsy water.

Gwen picked a thin book at random from the shelf. It was entitled *Legends and Myths*. She idly flicked through the densely written pages. Again for no reason she could clearly say, her mind was now on the book rather than on Tomas. One word caught her eye.

'Sleih,' she said.

Mark humphed. 'Sleih? That's the fairytale, not us.'

'Sleih?' Callie straightened in the chair. 'Isn't there a story that the Sleih helped us, the time the Madach drove us out?' Her eyes grew dark, thoughtful.

Gwen put the book on the floor. 'Ma! What do you know

about the Sleih?'

Meg wandered into the room, an oval platter in one hand, a cloth in the other.

'The mythical Sleih? Not much. Why? What have Sleih got to do with anything?' She snorted. 'Expecting them to help us out like they supposedly did last time?' She turned to go back to the kitchen and stopped, whirled about.

'Lucy,' she said. Her eyes glinted.

Gwen and Mark looked at each other.

Callie leaned towards Meg. Her eyes grew darker.

'The searchers who found Lucy's basket,' Meg said, 'told us there was a horse, which went west.' She waved the sudsy cloth in the air. 'Didn't the Danae come from the west, through the Deep Forest? Isn't the west where the Sleih would be?' She nodded hard. 'It must have been the Sleih who took Lucy. Someone should find the Sleih. See if they'll help us, if they exist. And,' she laughed, a little hysterically Gwen thought, 'we'll find our beautiful, darling Lucy with them.'

She gulped, tears filling her eyes, her excitement drained.

'They helped us, Ma?' Gwen said. She didn't want to talk about Lucy being with the Sleih. It seemed too far-fetched.

Meg sniffed. 'So the legends say. They also say they asked a high price in return, except no one knows what that price was. Or how they helped us.'

'Didn't work, whatever it was,' Mark said. 'The Madach still kicked us out.'

'Lucy,' Meg whispered, as if Lucy was already restored to her.

There was a short silence which the crackle of the fire broke, and with it Callie said, 'That's what you have to do, Gwen, Mark. That's what you have to do.'

'What are you talking about?' Meg said. She clutched the platter and cloth to her like they were a newborn baby.

'I've always said there's something each of us have to do.

Now I know what Gwen and Mark have to do. They have to find the Sleih. And Lucy.'

'And what do you have to do, Miss Mystery?' Mark said. But nicely. Not scornful.

'I don't know yet.'

'Are you suggesting me and Mark simply stride off into the Deep Forest,' Gwen said, 'traipsing west until we find these Sleih, or not, and Lucy, or not?' Gwen wondered at the tickle of anticipation settling in her stomach. It should have been dread at the thought of such a long, dangerous and hopeless quest.

'No.' Meg put the platter and cloth on a shelf and shook her head. 'You will do no such thing. We've already lost your father, and now Lucy. I won't risk the both of you too.'

'Hmm.' Mark stroked his chin like an old man might do. 'Miss Mystery might have a point,' he said. 'After all, it's a chance to get some help. A small one but a chance.'

'Then Tomas ...' Meg gulped a breath, went on. 'The Elders can send others, grown men who can tackle the dangers, find their way.'

'The grown men are needed here. To fight the Madach.' Callie said this in a way which suggested to Gwen there would be fighting. At some stage.

Gwen saw the green of Callie's eyes had deepened almost to black, the way they were when Callie woke from a nightmare. Gwen couldn't help gazing into them, and as she gazed she found herself saying, 'We have to go now, tonight.'

The idea was fixed in her mind. So simple. Why hadn't they already left? They should have been well on their way by now. She turned from Callie to grin at Mark. He too was watching Callie. He tore his eyes from Callie and returned Gwen's grin.

'We'll bring the king of the Sleih here, Ma, to throw these Madach into the sea!' Mark laughed out loud.

'Go now? Tonight? No!' Meg said. 'You're not going at all.'

Mark and Gwen stood side by side. Gwen hadn't known she could feel so certain about what had to be done. Maybe it was Callie's smiling encouragement, the way her darkened green eyes were searching Gwen's eyes, and Mark's.

Callie had a feel for these things. She'd been right about the Madach.

'Tomorrow will be too late,' Gwen said. 'It has to be tonight, while it's dark and they aren't watching us.'

'We hope they aren't watching us,' Mark said.

Meg fluttered her hands.

'No one else is looking for Lucy.' Callie's statement was flat and matter-of-fact. She shifted her green gaze to her mother, held Meg's eyes with her own.

Meg put her hands to her cheeks, drew in a huge breath.

'No.' She let the breath out.

Silence ticked for a second, two ... then, 'If you're all so determined ....' Meg gave Callie a tearful smile.

***

When Gwen had said 'Sleih', Callie's heart had beat faster.

Sleih, Sleih.

Hazy images of gorgeous kings and queens and ... young princes ... astride exquisite horses ... circled Callie's head like golden bees swarming around a hive.

The Sleih.

That was when Callie understood what it was Gwen and Mark had to do. And how, for reasons Callie couldn't explain even to herself, it was about Lucy too.

Was Meg right, about Lucy being with the Sleih? A pinch of discomfort pricked at Callie's brain, quieted again.

Gwen and Mark began to gather clothes and food and bits useful for a long journey through a dangerous Forest and roll them in blankets. Callie slid through the slimmest crack in the kitchen door and tiptoed outside to find out whether the Madach were watching or not.

No, she told the others when she returned, the Madach hadn't seen her. She'd seen them, however, in the dark lanes and alleys.

Madach sailors with sticks and soldiers with swords guarded the track east out of the village. That didn't matter because Mark and Gwen wanted to go west into the Forest and from there – west and west until they found the Sleih. There were Madach on that track too, and in the lanes between the cottages. The tapping of their sticks and swords on the hard dirt belied any idea they were out for casual evening strolls.

No Danae were about. Curtains were drawn across cottage windows. Doors were closed and no doubt bolted.

'How are we going to get away?' Gwen said.

She wore her cloak over a pair of Mark's trousers, and her stoutest boots. Her blanket roll was tied to her back with belts, and draped over each shoulder was a bag stuffed with what Meg considered the basic necessities for travelling through the Deep Forest. Mark was burdened with blankets and bags too.

If they were seen, their intent would be clear.

'I'll go first,' Callie said. 'Be a lookout for you.'

She grinned. 'And if they catch me, I'll scream and kick and wake the whole village and there'll be a huge confusion and you can get away.'

At Meg's frown, Gwen said, 'They won't punish a little girl for wandering around in the dark, Ma, surely not.'

***

They crept out the back door, sneaked around the cottage to the front. Callie hushed Gwen and Mark and stole to the track, squinting through the darkness. No moon tonight. The only light was what filtered through the curtained windows.

Callie wasn't fully certain about the Madach not being able to see her unless she wanted them to. Also, because she wasn't certain and because she didn't want to be laughed at, she hadn't confessed her possible talent to her family. Not yet.

Tonight it worked, though.

Callie peeked around corners and came face to face with Madach sailors who looked straight through her while she waved behind her for Gwen and Mark to stay where they were until Callie found a different way. The three of them tiptoed from wall to wall, tree to tree, huddled together, not speaking. The night was still and sound carried a long way. Callie worried Mark's excited breathing would give them away, or Gwen's gasp when the heavy bags she carried thudded into a fence.

It was a slow age before they came to the far edge of the village and the criss-cross of paths the Madach hadn't yet discovered.

'We'll be able to get away from here,' Gwen whispered.

She hugged Callie and Callie hugged a reluctant Mark.

'Stay safe,' Callie said. A thought came to her. It was to do with rabbits. 'The Forest creatures might help you.'

'The Forest creatures?' Mark quietly scoffed.

'It's more their Forest than ours,' Callie said. 'They must want these Madach to go away too.' Her mind skipped to the rabbit's sorrow at what the Madach had already done to its brothers and sisters. She took a deep breath.

Mark and Gwen faded into the trees, the last traces of them a soft crack of a twig.

'Find Lucy. Find the Sleih,' Callie whispered.

She wrapped her cape more tightly around her shoulders and hurried back to an anxious Meg.

90

Chapter Nineteen

One Village And A Wall

'Your senior Elder and myself believe,' Jarrow told the summoned villagers the next evening, 'it would be best if everyone was together in one village. The other one.'

He jerked a dirty thumb over his shoulder.

'Helps us keep a better eye out. Make sure no one wanders off and gets hurt.'

Elder Judith broke the amazed silence.

'Tomas has agreed to this?'

Her disbelieving question broke through the villagers' shock. Angry shouts rang through the square.

'Where is Tomas?'

'Why can't he tell us himself?'

'What have you done with our leader?'

Callie tugged at Meg's arm. 'Would have been hard for Gwen and Mark to escape,' she said.

Meg nodded, her mouth set. 'We'll be crowded like cows at milking.'

Jarrow waited until the shouts wore down to grumbles, head-shaking and sideways glances at the sword and stick-tapping Madach surrounding the villagers.

Families would have to move, he explained patiently, as if talking to babes. Everyone could take with them a few necessary belongings. For the time being, while the Madach were working in the forest, the bigger village would be closed to the Danae.

'For how long?' Matthew shouted from the far end of the square.

Jarrow ignored him.

He smiled the black smile. 'I can't emphasise enough how this is for your own safety.'

***

Meg piled clothes, bedding, and any food she hadn't given to Gwen and Mark, into two barrows. She left the barrows near the front door, took Callie's hand and led her through the kitchen into the garden.

The hens had already been rounded up and taken to their new home in the small village.

Callie's heart ached as Meg visited each vegetable bed in turn, pulling a few weeds, pricking out the new carrot tops pushing their way through the rich soil.

Finally, Meg stood back, hands on her hips. 'They should be all right,' she said, 'if we get enough rain. There'll be weeds when we get back, otherwise they should be all right.'

Callie nodded. The ache in her heart didn't ease.

They left the cottage, Callie pushing the lighter of the barrows, Ginger Cat curled on a pillow, asleep.

Mr and Mrs Biggs and their three children stood by the gate to their cottage, watching their neighbours walking by with their loaded carts.

'Aren't you leaving?' Meg said.

'No, we are not.' Mr Biggs set his hands on his wide hips. 'Who does this Jarrow think he is, pushing us out of our homes? Arrangements! Huh!'

Meg shook her head and kept walking.

Matthew and his wife Ella stood outside their white cottage. Ella was pleading tearfully with her husband. 'They'll push us out anyway. Why make it more difficult?'

Matthew glared down the lane, his muscled arms crossed.

Callie followed his gaze. Madach soldiers with drawn swords marched towards them. The straggling line of barrows and carts drew to a ragged halt.

'Come along, off you go.' The soldier waved the sword at Ella.

She cried out.

Matthew stepped into the path of the sword and glowered at the soldier. 'You won't win this, whatever it is you're up to.'

Another soldier marched the few steps to the cottage. He slammed a length of wood he'd been carrying across the closed door. A third nailed it to the frame.

'No!' Ella cried, and had to grip Matthew's arm to stop him flinging himself at the soldiers.

'Off you go,' the sword-waving Madach said.

Ella clasped her hands over her pregnant belly. 'Can't we get our things?'

'Too late.'

Those villagers who had watched the scene and weren't already pushing barrows, returned to their homes, including Mr Biggs.

Callie and Meg became part of a long line of families with wagons or barrows heaped with clothes and food and bedding, making their reluctant way along the track.

Like the story of the Danae forced from The Place Before. The thought ran over and over in Callie's head.

As each family reached the smaller village, they were herded by soldiers and sailors into the square. They stood about, their barrows and bags at their feet, asking each other what was happening and couldn't they get on to their new homes and unpack? Their neighbours, who were providing these new homes, joined them in the over-crowded square, encouraged there by the Madach.

A soldier called above the murmurings.

'Danae! Your attention please!'

Heads turned at the shout. The littlest children hid their faces in their mothers' skirts.

'Before you go off to your new places, we'd like you to line up in rows,' the soldier said.

The Danae didn't appear to understand. They stayed where they were.

'In rows.' The soldier gave his upright sword a quick twirl. 'Not too hard to do, is it?'

The Madach who had shepherded the Danae from the larger village, closed in to harry the villagers into lines. They pulled arms and shoved shoulders, herded people this way and that. The Danae's loud complaints were met with more pulling and shoving. Mothers tried to keep their children near. Younger people helped the older ones. Everyone tried to avoid the sailors' sticks and the soldiers' swords. The barrows and wagons got in the way and were kicked aside by the Madach. Clothes and pots and blankets lay strewn over the square's neat stones.

It took some time and a lot of fussing to line them all up – and then the Madach counted them.

Callie didn't want to be counted. She didn't know why.

You can't see me, she chanted inside her head. *You can't see me.*

Her heart beat hard but she was certain the Madach missed her.

After the count, the soldier who had told them to line up said, 'We'll do a count every evening. It's to make sure everyone's safe. We don't want anyone going off into the forest and getting hurt.' He curled his lips in the same joyless manner as Captain Jarrow. 'Have a happy evening settling in with your friendly neighbours.'

***

Meg and Callie and Ginger Cat moved in with the family of Mark's friend Jethro – mother and father, Jethro and two small girls.

Word spread that Gwen and Mark had escaped into the Deep Forest to find help of some sort. A handful of villagers scoffed at the idea of getting help from the mythical Sleih. Mostly however, they whispered soothing words to Meg, told her how brave her children were and it would surely be all right in the end. Meg thanked them.

Callie didn't mind the thin mattress on the floor. She was more worried what all this might mean. She could hear Meg talking with Jethro's parents late into the night, asking themselves how long the Madach meant to keep them all together and what the Madach were doing in the Forest.

She fretted over the rabbit. It might have come back, as Callie had asked it to do. And gone away. It wouldn't come again. Not when it thought Callie couldn't be trusted to keep her word.

***

The second evening in the small village, Captain Jarrow addressed the roundup in the square.

'Danae,' he said, 'thank you for your cooperation.'

He gave them the smile which never reached his slits of eyes.

'I know it's difficult, and I hope you won't all be crowded like this for long.'

The Madach either side of him exchanged quick grins. Few noticed. Most eyes were on Captain Jarrow, who was saying, 'I'm concerned about the children.'

Startled parents put their hands on the shoulders of their nearest child. Mothers looked askance at fathers.

'I worry that with all the work going on, it's not safe for the children outside the village. They need to be kept out of harm's way,' Jarrow said with a solemn nod.

The parents nodded too.

'I don't want to be responsible for any small Danae getting in the way of the tree-fellers, or falling down one of the holes my men are digging.'

More nodding.

'So, I believe we need a fence around the village, to stop the children wandering off and hurting themselves – or worse.' Captain Jarrow's lips curled.

The nodding stopped.

'How big a fence?' someone said.

'Big enough it can't be climbed over.'

Did he mean by the children or by anyone? Callie wondered.

'I would've had my own men build it,' Captain Jarrow said, 'if I had enough to spare.' He stared at the villagers. 'I don't. You Danae will have to build it.'

Matthew raised his voice over the confused grumblings. 'You're asking us to build our own jail?'

Captain Jarrow humphed at this suggestion. 'No, no. Not a jail.' He found the eyes of a young mother standing close to Callie, her toddler at her feet. 'It's to protect the little ones.' He glared at Matthew.

An Elder named James peered at Jarrow from beneath grey, hairy caterpillar eyebrows. 'We need time to talk this over.'

Jarrow shrugged. 'Talk if you wish, only talk about how it's going to be built, not whether it's going to be built.'

He didn't wait for any more. He strutted out of the square, his men on his heels.

The villagers watched them go. The Elders huddled in a small group. Callie edged close. She shared Matthew's fears about this wall.

Matthew joined the Elders. 'We can't do this,' he said. 'We can't imprison ourselves.'

Several mothers argued with Matthew. 'Who says it's a prison? They're talking about a fence, not a prison.'

'It's a good idea, it means we won't have to constantly watch the toddlers, worry about them.'

'Surely it'll have gates.'

'If we need a fence to keep the children safe, it must be built.'

Elder James agreed. 'True, although I suspect there's more to this fence than keeping the children safe. Still, what can we do about it?'

'Refuse to build it?' Matthew said.

'No,' Elder Judith said. 'We should do what they ask. They have swords, they're stronger than us.'

'Besides,' Elder James said, 'this Jarrow has promised to leave us be once they've finished here. I don't want to do anything which might make him change his mind.' He raised a hairy eyebrow at Matthew. 'Do you?'

'They could drive us out of the village altogether if they want to,' a young mother said. 'I'm not spending the winter wandering the Forest, not with three babies.'

'Yes,' another mother said. 'We should keep calm and hope we're safe until these Madach go home, wherever home is.'

Matthew threw up his arms. 'If Tomas was here, he'd show more spirit.'

Callie silently agreed. But Tomas wasn't there.

Tomas hadn't been seen since the day the soldier dragged him out of the village.

But, more spirit? Callie made a decision.

Chapter Twenty

The Secret Valley

Callie ran to where Madach soldiers stood on the track beyond the last cottage. They chatted while they kept an eye out for anyone who might want to leave the village. The farmers had already been escorted to their fields, the miller and Peter to the mill and Matthew to his forge. Everyone else was turned back, told it was too dangerous with all the work going on.

Callie waited until a small group of people gathered to argue with the soldiers about not being allowed into the Forest. She concentrated hard.

You can't see me. She kept her head down, walking steadily past. *Don't see me.*

The soldiers were ushering the arguing people back into the village. One drew his cloak a little closer as Callie passed, shivering as if a cloud had momentarily hidden the bright sun.

Callie ran towards the bigger village. Before she reached it, she took the track up to the ridge and down again into the Forest, to the place where she'd met the rabbit.

Of course, there was no rabbit there this time.

Callie slumped to the sparse grass under the willow and stared at the hanging branches' bright spring growth.

There was something she had to do. She knew there was. She scrunched up her eyes. Finding the Sleih was what Gwen and Mark had to do. What did she have to do?

Callie opened her eyes. The little stream burbled over its red and green stones, the bluebells shimmered in the hazy sunlight beneath the bright green of the new beech leaves, and yellow and white butterflies danced in the spring air.

What was it she had to do? Something to drive these Madach away. What?

Rat-a-tat-tat! sounded right above her. Callie peered up into the willow.

A woodpecker blinked at her before tilting its head to the edge of the cropped branches. Callie followed the movement and saw the rabbit, watching her. Her heart leaped.

It was just one rabbit, but it had come.

'Hello, rabbit.' Callie smiled.

The rabbit hopped closer and, nose twitching, ears back, concentrated hard on Callie's face. Callie screwed up her own nose to help her concentrate too.

Come. I know where there's help, Callie heard the rabbit say.

It was as if it was moments ago they'd last met, not days.

Help? Callie's excitement grew.

She climbed out from under the willow and followed the rabbit back up to the ridge, where it led her along a winding trail. From time to time it glanced back to make sure Callie was following.

They walked away from the inlet where the Madach ships were anchored, leaving the villages behind. Through the trees to Callie's left, the green ocean glinted, whitecaps sparkling. They walked for a long time and Callie was getting thirsty under the warming sun, when the rabbit veered off the path to wriggle through a rabbit-sized gap in the bushes.

Callie watched its white tail disappear. She pushed the bushes apart. Was the help she needed through here?

'Oh!'

Beyond the screen of greenery, the ground was unexpectedly bare. A wide, grassy slope opened to either side of Callie and down into a valley. Beyond the valley, the forested hills rolled into the distance, range after range until they were a smear of deep purple against the sky.

Callie gazed at the faraway hills. She thought of Gwen and Mark in that vastness, searching for the Sleih. A long and dangerous journey.

Despite the day's bright warmth, a thick white mist filled the valley below her. The rabbit, ears straight up, was skipping down the grassy slope into the mist, apparently expecting Callie to follow.

Callie hesitated. It'd be easy to get lost in that whiteness.

What sort of help was the rabbit expecting to find in the mist-filled valley? Wanting to know the answer to this question made up Callie's mind. She took a deep breath and plunged into the fog.

The thick white mist wasn't thick at all. But below its moist, shallow layer, Callie's familiar Forest was gone.

She and the rabbit stood on the side of a deep, wide natural bowl where green, pink and golden butterflies dipped and hovered above a tumult of gloriously coloured wildflowers. Mossy rocks, small ferns growing from beneath them, lay scattered at the bottom of the bowl. Grand old trees, their leaves glowing as if each one had been waxed and polished, grew in stately fashion between the rocks. Birds as bright as the butterflies darted between their branches.

Despite the mist above, it was sunnily bright in the grassy bowl. It was also quiet, except for the tumbling splash of water plunging down a crumbling yellow stone wall into a pool ringed with more of the yellow stones.

Callie pushed back her damp, dark curls, frowning. Was she dreaming?

She must have fallen asleep under the willow, waiting for the rabbit to come.

Remembering her thirst, she made her way to the pool, scooped up a handful of water and drank. The water tasted sweet.

The rabbit jumped onto the stones and drank alongside her.
Is it good?

'Very good.'

To the side of the pool, a red-flowering vine trailed over the ruins of a stone arch set against the steep slope of the grassy bowl. A dim light gleamed through the red flowers, suggesting the arch had once been the grand entrance to a cave.

The rabbit hopped to the arch, paused and looked back at Callie.

Come on. Help's here.

Imagining bears and wolves which lived in caves, Callie was reluctant to push the red-flowered curtain aside. The rabbit didn't hesitate. It skipped through as if expecting to greet an old and dear friend. Callie once more took her lead from the rabbit and stepped through after it.

An angry, yet weak, bird-like cry greeted her, followed by a smothered mewling. Callie stopped, one hand on the crumbling arch.

In the muted light from a hole in the rocky roof, she saw she was indeed in a wide cavern. Water dripped, splashing into a pool or a stream. The air was cold.

Callie waited to be able to see in the dimness. She wondered where the rabbit was.

The weak cry came again.

Callie started, and drew back at the sight of the huge beast which lay on its side on the hard-packed earth floor, its massive head facing her.

The beast's eyelids fluttered, a fierceness gleaming from dulled green eyes.

Not a bear or a wolf. Callie was still afraid.

She'd never seen an animal like this one. It had the neck and head of an eagle, although the feathers were a pale, sickly, blue.

Its body was like a large cat, or a lion, as in the picture Callie remembered seeing in a book from school. Her widened eyes travelled the beast's length to see the tail, long and muscled, tipped with a tuft of coarse white hair. One long dark wing closed against the lion body, another spread, all hollows and peaks like a feathered mountain range, on the floor of the cave. The beast's scaly front legs bore patchy tufts of the same blue feathers as its head. Massive talons slowly flexed.

The beast raised its head and opened its curved beak. Another weak cry came, this one no longer angry. Exhausted by the effort, the beast's head slumped to the floor.

Callie's fear fled. The poor, beautiful beast was ill. Rather than the beast helping her, Callie had to help the beast.

Callie. The beast spoke to her mind … hesitant, painful.

Callie's eyebrows rose. The beast knew her name?

We are gryphon … our fate, to guard … to wait … the treasure … until the time …

There was a long pause. Callie crouched by the eagle head, larger than her own head. She didn't dare touch it. She couldn't be so familiar with a beast as regal as this.

My destiny … not to see … The gryphon blinked, wearily, heavily, at Callie. *The child … his destiny, to see … take care … treasure.*

A translucent film hid the already faded green of the gryphon's eyes. Its eyelids closed, and did not open again.

Callie reached out, daring now to stroke the pale blue feathers. There was no movement from the gryphon. Callie knelt by the gryphon's head and quietly cried.

The rabbit pushed its head into Callie's lap.

Is she dead? The rabbit shuddered, as if it too was crying.

They stayed that way for some time, Callie with one hand on the gryphon's lifeless neck, the other on the rabbit's warm fur. A deep sadness grew inside her, gathering up her grief for her lost father and her lost sister with her grief for the gryphon.

Callie considered the gryphon's words. *Treasure?* She peered vaguely around the cave through blurred eyes. She couldn't see any treasure.

The mewling cry Callie had heard before came again, startling both her and the rabbit. Something moved on the other side of the dead gryphon. The wing which reminded Callie of a small mountain range was shifting.

Callie walked around the long body and found the child, hidden under the wing.

Not a Danae or Madach child. This was the gryphon's child. The baby gryphon mewled, crawled out from under his mother's wing and flopped at Callie's feet. Deep green eyes gazed up at her.

Callie couldn't help smiling at the plump bundle of tawny velvet fur with its skinny lion's tail which ended in a white bob whose size and fluffiness would make a rabbit jealous. Downy, palest silver blue feathers covered his head and his front legs. His stick-thin back legs sprawled behind him, as if they had nothing to do with the rest of him.

Although a baby, he was already half Callie's size.

The rabbit's pink nose twitched, its brown eyes fixed on the gryphon.

'You're too big for it to eat,' Callie said to the rabbit. The rabbit gave her a doleful look.

The baby gryphon – Child, Callie decided she would call him Child, as his mother had called him – heaved himself from the floor, wobbled for a moment on his mismatched and tremulous legs and tottered to the entrance of the cave. His feathered head pushed through the red-flowered vine, and there he stayed, as if the flowers held him tight.

Callie joined him, holding the vine's tendrils aside so they could all pass through.

Child gazed around, his baby eagle beak held high. He moved his head side to side to take in the grassy bowl. His eyes followed a bright bird and he lurched from the cave.

Callie and the rabbit watched him. Child opened his baby wings, gave them a few experimental flaps. He lifted his front legs, managed to bring his back ones under control, and stumbled a few steps, flapping the wings. With a grunt, he pushed himself into the air.

There he appeared graceful, at ease.

He flew around the bowl, growing in confidence, diving playfully at Callie and frightening the rabbit nearly to death by diving at it too before pulling up at the last moment and doing a roll.

Child flicked his long tail and soared upwards, through the white mist. Callie and the rabbit stared after him.

Chapter Twenty One

Paws And Claws

The rabbit and Callie climbed through the white mist to the ridge. At the top, Callie looked down into the grassy bowl.

The mist had gone. So had the grassy bowl. In its place was a treed valley like any other treed valley in the Forest. Callie frowned at the trees. Had she been dreaming? If so, she was awake now, trekking back along the ridge under the hot spring sun.

When she reached the willow tree she took a long drink from the stream, dabbed cool water on her face and rested within the tree's tented branches. The rabbit stretched beside her.

She should go home.

She was too tired to move. She wasn't hungry, although it must be past lunch. Her mother would be getting worried. The soldiers might want to know where she'd been.

Callie sighed and stayed under the tree.

The stuttering rat-a-tat-tat of a woodpecker made Callie flick open her eyes.

She pulled herself up straighter. The woodpecker wasn't alone this time. Robins, owls, buzzards, even a pair of eagles, jostled for space in the old branches of the willow, alongside a family of red squirrels which bumped into each other and the birds.

The rabbit gave an excited hop. It nudged Callie's knee.

Look.

Callie brought her gaze down from the tree. She clapped her hands to her cheeks, feeling her smile spreading wide.

A circle of nervous Forest creatures was gathering before her, tentative, poised to bolt should this all turn out to be a big mistake. Callie, her tiredness fled, made sure not to wriggle a finger for fear of scaring them away.

The badgers lined up at the front. Callie sensed their uneasiness, knew the adults were warning the little ones to stay close. She was uncertain whether this was to keep the babies safe from her, or from the foxes sitting at the edge of the group.

The largest of the foxes held himself haughtily. Callie heard his disdain, asking himself what this little girl could say that he didn't already know.

Callie stifled a delighted laugh. It wasn't only rabbits, and not just one rabbit, which she could understand. Her heart soared.

At the back of the group, barely within the hanging willow branches, a family of boar nuzzled at the earth. Deer stood alongside the boar, their round eyes questioning. Callie flinched from the swift vision of their losses from the invading Madach.

The eagles acted as lookouts, staring into the Forest rather than at the tempting sight of the tiny voles and field mice lined up at Callie's feet.

The torrent of the forest creatures' worries and fears and hopes washed through Callie's dizzy head.

The haughty fox blinked his amber eyes. *The Guardian has summoned us to you.*

'The Guardian?' Callie said to the rabbit. 'What does the fox mean?'

The rabbit twitched its nose. *The Guardian is dead, we saw her, in her valley. She's dead.*

'Do they know she's dead?'

The rabbit shrugged its furry shoulders. *It is not for you to tell. They will know when it is time to know.*

Our fate, to guard ... The gryphon's words. Is that what the dying beast meant to tell her? Did the gryphon guard the Forest? Was the Forest the treasure?

For a moment, Callie despaired. The rabbit had been right to take her to the secret valley. There had been hope. Now the hope had died.

Except ...

Callie didn't wriggle, despite her stiff knees. She didn't wave her hands and she spoke softly.

'Thank you for answering the summons of the Guardian,' she said. 'For some reason which I don't know, I can hear what you want to tell me. And you appear to understand me. At least, the rabbit does.'

The rabbit's ears went up.

'It's strange for all of us and I hope we can get used to it.'

A buzz of responses tickled Callie's mind. She waggled her head. Two of the mice scuttled back a step.

'Sorry.'

Callie gazed across the animals and up to the birds and squirrels. 'Our Forest is in danger,' she said, 'from these Madach, the people who've come on the ships.'

The wild creatures listened. Up in the branches, the squirrels stopped their chattering.

Callie understood, very well. As with her own people, homes and food were being heedlessly destroyed by these Madach, along with the trees.

The nightmare loomed. *The animals fleeing, their fear searing her mind ...the Danae at the edge of the Forest ...*

Callie's voice dropped to a whisper. 'I don't know what they have in mind, for the Forest, for all of us ...' The hissing monster beat against her skull. 'But I do know we have to stop them, before it's too late.'

A new rush of buzzing filled Callie's mind. Every furred and feathered face looked to her, hope in their eyes.

Callie slowly shook her head. 'No, I'm sorry. I can't make the Madach leave, not by myself.'

There was a shuffle of paws and claws, a ripple of movement like a wave of disappointment.

'If we have any chance of making these Madach go away,' Callie said, 'we have to work together, before they do worse things to our Forest.'

The boar nodded their huge heads. The deer huddled closer to each other.

'I've some ideas, if you're willing.'

The creatures watched, heads to the side, ears pricked, eyes bright.

'Let's make trouble for the Madach,' Callie said. 'As much trouble as we can, in any way we can. If we make their life impossible, they might give up and go back to wherever they came from.'

The boar kept nodding, pawing at the earth as if they wanted to dig the Madach into it. The rabbits' long ears were erect. Strong back legs thumped.

Callie gave an excited jiggle, happy to see the mice didn't scatter this time. 'You boar could dig up their potatoes.' She squinted up into the leaves. 'You squirrels could steal things from their ships, and you mice,' Callie smiled at the tiny creatures, 'could eat their food.'

Did they understand?

'Because you're animals, you'll be able to do lots of things we Danae can't do. And if the Madach see you, they'll think it was simply wild creatures being wild creatures.'

Their excitement dampened.

Callie shuddered at the images in the forest creatures' heads of what the invaders would do to stop them digging potatoes or stealing things or eating Madach food.

For a moment Callie faltered, before her nightmares clamoured the fate of all the creatures if these Madach stayed.

'There's something else,' she said. She wanted to let the animals know it wasn't all up to them and so she told them about Gwen and Mark journeying through the Deep Forest to find the Sleih and ask for help.

The wild creatures knew nothing of the Sleih. They did know, however, of the dangers of the Deep Forest.

'I wondered,' Callie said, 'if you could spread the word about my brother and sister, ask others to keep an eye on them, look after them?'

The haughty fox blinked and slipped away. Two young boar trotted after the fox. And one of the eagles flew off, its wide wings causing a robin to nearly topple from its branch.

Fewer animals remained now. The deer had gone. Many of the rabbits too, no doubt remembering little wooden cages. The badgers, the boar and the foxes were still there, and up in the branches the squirrels flicked their bushy tails and the birds fluttered their wings as if anxious to get started. The mice squatted on their tiny haunches at Callie's feet, waiting for their orders.

Callie was about to say thank you, when something big and tawny, with silvery pale blue feathers, landed with a thud on the ground. The creatures fell silent.

Child tried to stand. He fell onto a sow who supported him while he sorted out his mismatched feet. Once he was upright, Child lifted his downy eagle head, opened the curved beak and gave a squeaky cry.

Then an odd thing happened.

The boar stretched out their fat front legs and lowered their heads between their dainty hooves. The badgers arched their backs, their snouts to the ground. The foxes knelt, heads tucked between their forelegs. The birds fluffed out their wings.

In their various ways, all the creatures bowed to Child.

Child's eagle head bobbed shyly, green eyes half closed. His beak glowed a soft rose colour.

The animals parted as Child stumbled to Callie and opened his beak in what Callie took to be a smile.

Callie peeked at the rabbit, which had its eyes fixed on the gryphon.

Child dropped at Callie's feet, and went to sleep.

A loud sigh arose from the gathered creatures.

The rabbit gave a hop and Callie looked at it, questioning.

Yes, the rabbit said, *now they know the Guardian is dead. They will grieve.*

In pairs and groups, the wild creatures melted into the Forest. The rabbit went with them. The birds flew off. The squirrels were hushed as they tumbled down the willow's trunk and scampered into the trees.

Callie stroked the sleeping Child's silver feathers. She thought about the words of the dying gryphon.

The child ... his destiny, to see ... take care ... treasure ...

What was the treasure? What was Child's destiny?

It was some time before Child woke. He didn't look at Callie. He stretched his wings and flew off above the Forest, towards the ridge.

Callie realised anyone watching from the village, or the ships, would wonder at this strange bird. She must tell him not to go near either, especially the ships.

If she saw him again.

***

Callie kept a tired eye out for wandering Madach as she wound her way back to the village. Once, she jumped at the too close thwack of an axe on wood and, as she grew nearer the Forest above the Madach ships, she sniffed smoke.

The sun was high, although most of the day must have passed. Callie was hungry, and anxious.

Meg would be angry.

She sneaked past the soldier guards, muttering, *Don't see me*, and sidled into Jethro's family's cottage.

Meg was at the kitchen cupboard, pulling out plates. Jethro's mother was laying food on the table. She looked up and smiled at Callie.

'There you are, Callie.' Meg waved at the food. 'Right on time for lunch. Go and get cleaned up.'

Callie's mouth opened. She shut it.

Chapter Twenty Two

Thinking

In line with the measurements given them by the ship's carpenter, the Danae built a sturdy fence around the village. It was much higher than anything needed to keep the children out of the Forest.

Madach soldiers and sailors patrolled the outside to 'make sure no one wandered off and got hurt'. There was one gate, and those working in the fields or the mill or smithy were allowed out each day in a group, escorted by Madach to their place of work and escorted back to the village at the end of the day.

The Madach said this was for the Danae's safety. The Danae understood they were prisoners, although for what reason they didn't know. Matthew, to his credit, reminded no one about his protests at having to build their own jail.

Tomas had not returned.

Elder James asked a Madach guard what had happened to Tomas. He was told Tomas was 'working with the captain on a mutually agreeable plan'.

The Danae, crowded in their cottages, unable to go beyond the wooden fence, went about their tasks with brows furrowed, heads down. The adults whispered when they spoke. The children fell quiet, the excitement of the move and being with their friends turning stale in the confined village. School was out as there was nowhere roomy enough to hold all the students.

During the long, boring days, Callie worried about what was happening to the forest creatures and if they'd been able to make the Madachs' life miserable. The meeting under the willow hadn't gone so far as to talk about what they could do. Callie fretted. She thought about trying to leave the walled village. However, walking along a track when it didn't matter if she was caught was very different from deliberately disobeying Captain Jarrow. A few young men and women had tried to sneak through the gate, pleading the need to collect firewood when they were caught. They'd been marched back to their homes and told, with smirking leers, that a second attempt would bring some unspecified punishment.

In the long nights, Callie tossed and cried out on her thin mattress and each night Meg cradled the one child she had left to her until both fell into an exhausted sleep.

Spring passed and early summer warmth promised hot days ahead. The Madach didn't leave or give any sign of leaving. None of the Danae knew what was happening in the Forest over the ridge towards the sea. Nor what was happening to Tomas, or how any 'mutually agreeable plans' were progressing.

Callie found Meg in tears one day.

'I'm glad Gwen and Mark are out of this,' Meg said. 'Let's hope they're safe, and let's hope they find the Sleih and get rid of these Madach for us.'

That evening, at the roundup, Callie stood close to Meg. She concentrated hard on not being seen, as she did every roundup.

You can't see me, you can't see me.

The Madach counted past her. Like every roundup.

Later, Callie perched on the wooden bench outside the cottage, stroking Ginger Cat sprawled across her lap, and putting off the time when she would have to go to bed. She knew the towering, hissing monster of her nightmare would be waiting, crouched in a hidden corner, ready to claw its way into her sleep.

Even here, outside in the red evening light, its terrifying presence loomed in her head … *smoke and steam billowing about her, engulfing the animals running alongside…* She gazed unseeing at the stones in the wall opposite, dragging her mind from the darkness of the dream.

She thought about Child. She sighed. Was the baby gryphon lonely, with no mother and no one to keep him company? Callie hoped he'd found a new home, with the Forest creatures.

Callie recalled for the hundredth time the strange gathering under the willow, smiling at the memory of the boar nodding their huge heads, eager to make mischief for the Madach, and the haughty fox which had slipped away. Hopefully, to let other wild creatures know about Gwen and Mark. At least she might have achieved some help for her brother and sister, if nothing else.

And what was the rabbit doing? Did the rabbit have a home anymore, or had the Madach destroyed its family's burrows? Callie bit her lip.

She remembered she'd met the rabbit the day she spoke to the Madach, the one who might be a good Madach. What was his name? Sir Tristan, the labourer had called him.

A good Madach.

Callie straightened up on the bench. Of course!

But how to get out of the village?

***

'Excuse me, Sir Tristan.'

Tristan squashed himself to one side of the narrow passageway to make room for Wilf, the cook's boy, passing by with a tray of cold venison and ship's biscuit.

'Supper for the prisoner,' Wilf said. 'Not that he'll eat it, hardly eats at all.'

'Here, give it to me. I'll take it to him.'

Tristan had no idea what made him say it. He'd spent the last weeks trying not to think about the Danae, captive in their village, another conquered people. And now he was offering to confront their imprisoned leader.

'Not your job, Sir Tristan, to carry food to prisoners. What'd Captain Jarrow say if I let you in with prisoners?'

The mention of Captain Jarrow steeled Tristan's resolve. 'Not up to Captain Jarrow to tell me what to do, is it?' he said in his haughty I'm the son of Lord Rafe voice.

He took the tray and walked down the passageway.

Wilf shrugged. 'The key's on the tray. Mind he don't escape!'

Tristan could feel Wilf staring after him until he reached the prisoner's door. He glared over his shoulder. Wilf shrugged again and wandered off to the galley.

Tristan set the tray on the floor, knocked, called, 'Supper!' unlocked the door, picked up the tray and pushed the door open with his foot.

The Danae leader was standing by the porthole, staring at the new wharf. He didn't turn as Tristan entered.

Tristan eyed the man's dark brown hair, curling to his stiffly set shoulders.

Another conquered people. A vision of little Alfred being hauled across the icy terrace passed before Tristan's eyes. The stifled memories of the dead-eyed workers in Lord Rafe's manufactories, of wailing women and tiny, lifeless bundles surged through his whirling head. He let the tray drop to the scratched table with a clatter.

What was he doing here? He slunk back to the door.

'Wait.'

Tristan waited, obeying the authority in the quiet voice.

The Danae leader had faced about to examine Tristan from top to toe. Tristan averted his flaming face from a pair of piercing midnight blue eyes that searched the depths of his soul.

'You're not the cook's boy. Who are you?'

'I'm Tristan.'

'And what's your part in this expedition, Tristan?'

'Umm, I'm on the expedition because, because ...' Tristan couldn't tell the Danae leader he was Lord Rafe's son. 'I'm here to survey the trees, write reports.' He hoped his apologetic tone would go unnoticed.

'Survey the trees? Before Jarrow cuts them all down? To make a record of what used to be here?'

Tristan knew he should bridle at this and tell the impertinent prisoner to hold his tongue. Instead, he shuffled his feet.

The blue eyes kept their fierce gaze on Tristan's face.

The Danae leader didn't move from his place by the porthole. 'You look like a bright young man,' he said. 'I've seen you coming and going along that... that thing your captain is building out there.' He waved at the wharf.

Tristan was silent, spellbound by the blue eyes.

The Danae leader blew out a long breath. 'Could you tell me what's happening, in the village? Is everyone safe?'

Tristan's head swarmed with pictures of the enslaved peoples of his father's empire, and of the Danae in their fenced-in village and of the fate which awaited them. A heavy sympathy filled him. He found it easier to meet the Danae leader's gaze.

'Yes, they're safe. There's a fence around the village. It's to stop people going into the forest and getting hurt while the work's going on.'

Tristan knew this wasn't the reason for the fence, but he wanted to reassure this leader who had lost his people.

'A fence?' The Danae leader frowned. 'To keep everyone in?'

He took a step forward and touched Tristan's arm.

Tristan wasn't afraid. 'Yes,' he said.

And couldn't say anything more, although a dozen things sprang to his spinning mind, including, You must escape, get your people away, before it's too late.

'Sir Tristan? What are you doing here?'

Captain Jarrow's frizzled ginger beard thrust its way through the doorway. His opaque eyes flickered from Tristan to the Danae leader.

'Master Tomas!' Captain Jarrow said. 'No conversations with the crew is what we agreed.'

He scowled at Tristan. 'What would your lord father have to say about you feeding prisoners, hey, Sir Tristan?'

Tristan tried to be haughty and lordly. Until he saw the creased brow of Master Tomas and grew hot instead.

Now the Danae leader knew who Tristan was. He would hate Tristan and would never talk to him again.

Tristan didn't say anything, not trusting his voice to stay steady. The best he could do was hold his head high as he pushed past Captain Jarrow into the passageway. He heard the key turn in the prisoner's lock behind him.

Those piercing eyes still reached into his soul.

Chapter Twenty Three

Tristan Decides

Callie wrapped her cape around her shoulders, quietly opened the cottage door and ran through the chilly dawn to the miller's house. It wasn't the miller she wanted to see. It was his son, Peter. Callie liked Peter. He always had time for Callie and her friends, happy to kick a ball with them for a moment or two, or fetch the same ball from the high branches of a tree.

Callie knew Peter had spent many many hours searching the Forest for Lucy when she disappeared. He would come by the cottage at the end of every day to tell Meg where he'd been and to ask if there was anything else he could do, was there any place he hadn't searched?

Most importantly, Peter worked at the mill with his father, so he was one of the Danae allowed through the gate each day.

Callie tapped her foot to keep warm, waiting for signs of waking inside before knocking on the door and asking to see Peter.

'It's very, very important.'

Peter stumbled down from the family's sleeping room, pale yellow hair ruffled from his pillow, brown eyes half-open.

'Why do you want to see me, Callie, and why so early?' A yawn escaped. 'I could've had another ten minutes sleep.'

Peter's mother went outside to fetch water and Callie hurriedly explained her plan.

'Mmm,' Peter said. 'Not sure your ma would be happy. Why

do you want to anyway?'

'I think I know where we might get help.'

'Help? You mean against these Madach?'

'Yes.'

'What kind of help?'

Callie had no chance to answer as Peter's mother came back in with the heavy kettle, placed it on the stove and said, 'I need you to fetch wood please, Peter.'

She looked at Callie. 'Are you staying for breakfast, Callie?'

'No, thank you, ma'am. Ma'll be expecting me.'

'Not sure it's a good idea,' Peter whispered, bending to pick up the basket for the wood.

'It probably won't work anyway,' Callie whispered back. 'They're bound to stop me at the gate, so what's the harm?'

Peter shrugged as he slouched towards the back door. 'All right. And don't blame me when you get into trouble with *them*.'

Callie reached home in time to avoid Meg asking where she'd been. She tried to calmly eat her breakfast.

***

They headed to the gate, where two guards counted the outgoing Danae.

Don't see me, don't see me, Callie chanted in her head. She stayed close to Peter.

The villagers gave her questioning frowns. Peter shook his head, and they said nothing.

They had to slow as they reached the gate, with the Danae bunching up inside. Callie's heart was in her throat. She waited for the call, 'Hey there, where are you going?'

It didn't come. The guards ignored her.

They were through.

Callie twisted around, saw the guards with their backs to them, grinned at Peter and mouthed, 'It worked'.

Peter didn't grin back. His forehead creased. Callie kept

grinning as she ran into the trees at the side of the track.

***

A hot stillness had replaced the chill of dawn. Callie stopped to catch her breath. She sniffed the smoky air and wrinkled her nose. A pall of grey ash hung over the Forest.

... the ash-laden air ... the animals' fear ...

She searched for her familiar ways between the trees. They were gone, buried beneath the jagged branches of felled trees, trampled into mud by heavy Madach boots, or one more strip of earth in a new field.

The Madach laboured among the scorched trunks and burnt grasses of areas already cleared, piling up logs, burning brush, building fences or digging over new fields. The thwack of hammers on posts and the clang of axes slashing the trees smothered any birdsong that might have been in the air.

A heaviness settled in Callie's stomach. The nightmare clawed at her mind...*the scarred desolation of torn stumps ...smoke billowing about her, engulfing the animals running alongside...*

She wandered in the devastation, from one horror to the next, forgetting she should hide from the Madach.

There were signs the Forest creatures were fighting back. A small machine lay on its side on a new track, dented, one wheel hanging at a strange angle. Lines of string, possibly marking off areas about to be cleared, were broken, the ends a tangled mess strewn between holly trees and brambles.

Passing by a muddy field, Callie saw a few neat rows of tender new potato plants waving their green tendrils where once wood anemones and bluebells had spread. The rest of the field was a churned up mess of shallow holes and dug over earth. Seed potatoes were scattered everywhere.

The boar. Callie hoped they enjoyed the seed potatoes.

A lump came to her throat at the image of the birds and animals striking where they could, trying in every way they knew to slow the Madach's destruction.

Two men were at work in the field. One raked the clods of earth, gathering the remains of the potatoes into a basket as he went from row to row. The other pounded in new fence posts.

The fencing man glanced Callie's way, stood up straight and called to his fellow worker. He pointed at Callie.

You can't see me, you can't see me, Callie breathed. She shrank behind a young larch, daring to peek out.

The men cast around in all directions, until the second one pushed the one who had spotted her. He threw back his head and guffawed. 'Goblins indeed!'

Callie turned from the ruined field and set her mind to searching for the Madach she wanted.

He was nowhere Callie looked. She crept close to the ships, muttering, *You can't see me,* and hoping by the Beings the incantation truly did make her invisible.

A very big area along the rocky shore had been scraped completely clean and the earth packed tight its full length and width. Posts that appeared to be made of smooth stone squatted like hunchbacked giants right at the sea's edge, the two ships tied to them with ropes as thick as Callie's legs.

A wharf, Callie realised, remembering her father joking about building one in the same place to tie up his tiny fishing boat.

These Madach had no plans to leave soon, if ever.

The Madach Callie wanted was nowhere near the ships. He might be on one of them, but neither Callie's courage nor her trust in her incantation was strong enough to find out.

She could be in the Forest all day and not find him.

Not knowing what else to do, Callie made her way to the willow where she'd met with the animals and birds. The Madach hadn't reached this place with their axes and saws and the air was clear.

She drank from the cool stream, took off her boots and

dabbled her feet in the water. She thought hard about the rabbit.

And it came, hopping slowly out from the ferns.

The rabbit's dulled eyes accused her. *Where have you been?*

'I'm sorry,' Callie said. 'The Madach are keeping us prisoners in the village.'

The rabbit's ears were down. Its fur was ragged and patchy, as if it no longer had the will to groom itself.

'What's happened?' Callie said.

The rabbit closed its eyes. Callie wept as she saw the flight of the rabbits, the Madach digging through their burrows, the adults rounding up the struggling kittens, pushing them to keep moving, fast, as fast as they could, along the tunnels, deeper into the earth.

'I'm sorry.' Callie wiped her tears with the edge of her ash-smudged dress.

The rabbit blinked. *Can you help?*

Callie sighed. 'I don't know what I can do.'

The rabbit's nose twitched. It kept its gaze on Callie's face.

'I do have an idea,' Callie said, 'which might work. I don't know.'

The rabbit hopped a step or two closer, one ear up, listening.

'I need to find one of the Madach. He might help. He's the one I saw the same day I rescued you from the cage. Not the one who had the cage. This one's tall, with curly brown hair. He walks around staring up all the time, like he's admiring the trees. Do you know the one I mean and where he might be?'

The rabbit pricked up its ears. Yes, it knew the Madach she meant. This Madach didn't chop down trees or burn them like the other Madach. Callie gathered this Madach preferred those parts of the Forest where his fellows had not yet ventured.

Good. Callie might be right about him being a good Madach.

Her request gave the rabbit new energy. It took off fast through the Forest.

'Wait!'

122

Callie struggled up and out from the willow's branches. The rabbit slowed, hopping ahead of her. It hesitated when they passed Madach tracks and burned out patches of Forest and jumped and skipped from bush to bush. Callie kept a careful watch, dodging this way and that like the rabbit.

The rabbit led her down towards the ocean and across the Forest to an area quiet and dark beneath summer-leaved trees. At last it stopped in a dappled clearing scattered with lichen-covered stones. It thumped one foot, and scampered off. Callie perched on a mossy stone, breathless and hot, and waited.

She didn't wait long.

A tall Madach with curly brown hair approached, head down, hands behind his back.

You can see me, can't you? Callie whispered. She feared the young Madach would walk straight past her.

At the last moment he halted mid-step, squinted, and stopped altogether.

'Hello, again,' Callie said.

The Madach gaped at her.

'You're one of the Danae,' he said. 'How did you get here?'

Callie shrugged.

'You shouldn't be here.' The Madach frowned. 'It's dangerous, there are lots of people about and trees being cut down and holes in the ground. You could get hurt.'

The Madach stopped talking and stared, as if he wasn't sure she was actually there.

Callie stared back.

'We've met before, haven't we?' The young Madach sounded uncertain. 'Wild mint. A sprig of wild mint. I'd forgotten. It was you, wasn't it? Did you cast a Danae spell on me?'

His frown deepened. Callie worried he might think she was a wicked goblin. She didn't want him believing she was wicked, not at all.

'No, no, I didn't cast a spell on you. I don't know what

happened. You could see me, and then you couldn't. I don't know why you couldn't remember. It wasn't anything I did, honest.'

He narrowed his eyes at her.

'What's your name and why are you down here in all of this?'

'Callie. I've been searching for you.'

'Why? Why are you searching for me?'

'Because I think you're a good Madach and you might help us.'

He didn't say anything. He kept looking at her. Callie wished she could tell what was in his head, like she could with the animals and the birds.

'Help you? Help the Danae?' he said at last.

'And the animals,' Callie said. 'Everyone's suffering and it shouldn't be happening. We're prisoners in our own village and Tomas is gone and we don't know what we can do or what's going to happen to us all.'

The young Madach stayed silent for a long time. When he did speak, Callie's hopes crumpled around the edges.

'I have to tell you,' he said, 'I don't have a lot of say about what goes on here.' It sounded to Callie like an excuse. 'It's my job to count the trees. Oh, and write reports, the boring bit.'

Callie pulled at a hanging black curl. The good Madach might be good, but he wasn't turning out to be much of a hero.

'Can't you see this is all too much? You Madach are destroying the whole Forest! Where will the creatures live? And what will your Captain Jarrow do with the Danae when he's finished here? If he's truly going to leave us alone, why are we being kept in a prison? And where's Tomas, what's Jarrow doing with him?'

***

Tristan's mind spun like the eddies of dust which spiralled over

Lord Rafe's desolated wildernesses. Since his first visit, when he'd gone with Jarrow to investigate the cause of the deer hunter's excitement, he'd avoided the Danae village. He didn't want to waken his sympathies for the conquered peoples of Lord Rafe's empire. Not when he could do nothing about it.

Then he had, foolishly, talked to their imprisoned leader. The encounter with the Danae leader had left him restless and uneasy. At night, his dreams were haunted by workers toiling in the steam and heat, by shabby, down-trodden clerks and starving babies. By day, he shivered in the summer sun at the memory of desolate plains where icy winds blew unimpeded, and always he nursed a deep sickness in his stomach as he saw, time after time, little Alfred dragged across the frozen archery ground.

Now he was staring into the eyes of a young girl from another conquered people. The green depths of those eyes would drown him in guilt. He turned his head away.

'You're right, I know,' he said, more to himself than the girl. 'What can I do? Jarrow doesn't listen to me. Anyway, he's too taken up with getting his wharf built, his machines put together and filling his ships with timber and fairytale Danae.'

Tristan stopped. How much had he said out loud? He drew back, blinking at the Danae girl.

'Oh!' She clutched at her chest, eyes wide. 'A fairytale come to life … a fairytale …'

Tristan's heart thudded at the girl's intensity.

She rose from the mossy stone, put her hands on her hips and glared at him.

'What do you mean, filling his ships with fairytale Danae? I knew he was lying! Where will he take us? What will become of us?'

Eyes danced in Tristan's head. Alfred's laughing eyes, the dead eyes of the manufactory workers, Tomas' soul-searching eyes, Jarrow's pale, calculating eyes. And the glinting black eyes of his father, narrowed in disdain at Tristan's many shortcomings.

In the shadowy clearing, the Danae girl's sea-green gaze outshone them all.

'You're our one chance,' she said.

Tristan drew in a deep breath and forced himself to gaze back, to look, properly look, at this young girl who would soon be separated from everything and everyone she knew to become the put upon 'playmate' of a Madach lord's brat.

Could he let that happen, without protesting? Could he brave his father's wrath?

'I don't know what I can do.'

Tristan's stomach somersaulted in confusion. The green eyes burned his skin.

The frozen archery ground seared his vision. Alfred's plaintive cries pained his ears.

Tristan's stomach settled. He returned Callie's stare.

'I'll try though.'

A smile!

'Because you're right, Callie. I know you're right.' Tristan's eyes filled. 'Maybe,' he said, 'just maybe, between us we can do something about it.'

Her smile grew wider. 'Your name's Sir Tristan, isn't it?'

Sir Tristan? He didn't bother to ask how she knew this.

'Yes, although simply Tristan will do, at your service, ma'am.'

Chapter Twenty Four

How Does It Help?

'What's young Callie up to? Why didn't the guards stop her?'

Their Madach escort was a good way behind them when Peter's father asked the question.

Peter shrugged. 'She says she might be able to find a way of helping us.'

His father snorted. 'She does? Where? Young Callie has too much imagination.'

Peter kicked at a stone in the track. 'I don't know. She acted all mysterious when she came by this morning.' He thought about their unchallenged passage through the gate. 'I thought they'd stop her and send her back. Don't know why they didn't.'

Later, sitting in the sunshine by the mill pond eating lunch, Peter said, 'Dad, there's something doesn't make sense here. Why are the Madach keeping us prisoners when they could drive us away, like they did from The Place Before?'

'No idea, Peter, and yes, it worries me too, although I'm not sorry they haven't driven us out.' His father took another bite of his pasty, chewed and swallowed it. 'Me and Matthew were talking in the inn the other night. He's all for a rebellion, rise up against these Madach and try and fight them off.' He gave a grim laugh. 'Much good we'd do, against those swords and knives they wave about.'

'Shouldn't we do something, not wait for whatever might happen?'

'Don't know what we'd do, at least not anything which

wouldn't make things worse.' Peter's father hoisted himself up from the grass with a long sigh. 'Back to work is all we can do, keep the villagers in bread, eh?'

***

The afternoon passed, work was over for the day and his father had already left the mill.

Peter swept the floor with abnormal care, counted the sacks of grain waiting for the next day's milling, sorted the different flours. He lingered by the door, waiting for the last summons to return to the village, hoping to give Callie as much time as possible to meet him by the gate.

A soldier poked his head around the doorway. 'Time to head back, you'll be late.'

Peter took a long time to close and bolt the heavy door. Afterwards, he ambled up the track, pretending to enjoy the mild evening, in no rush to return to the over-crowded village. The soldier strolled behind him.

They reached the fence. Peter slowed, slowed, slowed ... A small hand touched his arm.

'Don't look down,' Callie said.

Then they were through the gate and into the square.

'Thank you, Peter.' Callie walked away, her shoulders slumped.

Where was the cheery Callie who dashed off into the Forest this morning, Peter wondered?

'Hold on,' he said. 'Why can't the Madach see you?'

Callie glanced at him. 'They just can't, unless I want them to.' Her voice was flat, dulled.

It wasn't really an answer, but Peter had another question. 'What did you do out there in the Forest? Did you find the help you were after?'

Callie wrinkled her nose. 'Yes, I did. I think.'

Before he could ask more, Peter caught sight of Meg striding towards them. Her face led him to melt into the crowd

128

docilely lining up in the square, leaving Callie to deal with what promised to be a fierce scolding.

***

Throughout the count, Callie glanced from time to time at Meg. Meg's lips were quivering. When their line was finished, Meg pulled Callie to the side of the square.

'Where have you been all day, Callie? You haven't been in the village, I know. I searched everywhere.' She drew Callie closer, sniffing at her straggling curls. 'Why do you smell of smoke? What have you been doing?'

Callie sniffed too, trying to think how to answer all these questions.

Meg didn't wait for any answers, however. Her voice trembled. 'Please, Callie, you mustn't disappear for hours at a time, you're all I have left. What if the Madach find you outside the village? What will they do to you?'

'I'm sorry Ma, sorry to worry you. It was really important, and I should have told you first, but you might not have let me go and I wouldn't have met Tristan and I wouldn't have found out about Tomas.'

'Tristan? Who's Tristan?' Meg kept frowning. 'You know where Tomas is? Is he okay? Is he safe?'

'Yes, he's safe. He can't come back to us, though, not yet anyway.'

Callie took her mother's hand. 'Let's go home. I can tell you about it there.'

After supper, Meg and Callie wrapped themselves in light shawls against the cooling night air and settled on the bench beside the cottage wall. The night was bright with stars, and quiet except for the hooting of a distant owl and, through the window of the cottage opposite, the clink of supper dishes being washed.

'How did you get out today?' Meg said. 'Why didn't they stop you?'

Callie pulled a wry face. 'They can't see me, not unless I

want them to.' She didn't mention Peter. Why should he be in trouble too?

Meg snorted. 'Sounds like a fantasy to me. I suggest they didn't notice and you were lucky.'

Callie didn't argue. She wanted her mother's help.

'Who's Tristan?' Meg said.

'He's a Madach whom I saw once before.' Callie left out when and where that was. 'He seemed to me to be a good Madach. I found him today and I was right. He'll help us.'

'Why? Why would a Madach help us?'

'Because,' Callie said, 'he doesn't like their plans for the Forest any more than we do.' Callie hunched forward on the bench, clutching the edge. 'You should see what they're doing to the Forest, Ma.' She shook her head, dark curls falling across her face. 'It's awful, too awful, and the wild creatures …'

Meg patted Callie's hand.

They were silent for a time, until Callie was able to say, 'Tristan loves trees. He doesn't want them all cut down.'

'How can he help us?' Meg's voice was soft.

'We don't know, yet. Someone needs to talk to the Elders, make them come up with a plan. If we have one of the Madach on our side we might have a chance of driving them out of here.'

'Mmm, perhaps.'

Callie wasn't sure whether the 'perhaps' referred to Tristan, the Elders or any plan which might have a chance of success.

'Tell me about Tomas. What's happened to him?'

'He's a prisoner on one of their ships. Jarrow told him we wouldn't be driven out of the Forest if he agreed to stay on the ship.'

'I see. Make us leaderless.'

'Yes. He can't come ashore and if he escapes Jarrow has said he'll burn down our village, make us all live in the ruins.'

Meg's eyes grew round. 'Burn down the village?'

She grabbed Callie by the shoulders to stare into her face.

'Callie, listen to me.' Meg's eyes glittered. 'We need to tell the Elders about Tomas. But, please listen to me, you must never go out of the village. You mustn't even think about doing anything to upset these Madach. If something happens, the Beings only know what they'll do to us.'

Callie wanted to say, You should hear the rest of it.

She couldn't, though. Meg had too much to worry about, with Lucy, Gwen and Mark gone, not knowing where they were and whether they would ever find their way home. Callie couldn't add to Meg's burdens.

Chapter Twenty Five

Machines

Forbidden their ornately carved chamber in the bigger village, the Elders had taken to meeting in the village inn. Meg hustled Callie into the low-ceilinged room where Elders Judith and James waited at an ale-stained table.

Elder James fidgeted with a piece of paper, sighing from time to time.

Elder Judith inclined her head in greeting. 'Now, Callie,' she said, 'we've been told you want to tell us something.'

Callie grew hot. She looked to Meg for encouragement.

'Go on,' Meg said. 'Tell Elder Judith and Elder James what you told me.'

Callie stuck her chin out. 'Yes, I do want to tell you something.' She found it hard to think under the Elders' scrutiny. 'The Madach can't see me unless I want them to. I'm sure they never count me at the roundup.'

The two Elders looked at each other.

Elder James folded the piece of paper in half. 'So?'

'I met a Madach in the Forest, the day I rescued the rabbit from the cage, and I thought he was a good Madach.'

Elder Judith gazed at Callie without blinking. Elder James' spiky grey eyebrows went up. Meg frowned.

Callie remembered she hadn't told her mother about the rabbit. Or Child.

She hurried on. 'Yesterday, I sneaked out and found my

good Madach. I asked him if he'd help us. He said he would.'

Now Elder Judith's eyebrows rose.

Meg squeezed Callie's arm. 'Tomas,' she said. 'About Tomas.'

Callie didn't want to go straight to talking about Tomas.

'We have to make a plan, and my good Madach will do whatever we need him to do so we can get rid of Captain Jarrow and his soldiers and woodcutters.'

The faces of the two Elders were blank.

'And the wild creatures will help.'

As soon as it was out, Callie knew it was the wrong thing to say.

Elder James pounced. 'The wild creatures?' The hairy caterpillar eyebrows threatened to fly from his forehead.

'What wild creatures?' Meg said.

Callie looked straight at the smirking Elder James. 'The Forest creatures can understand me, and I can understand them. They don't actually talk to me. That would be strange.'

Elder James gave an exasperated sigh.

Meg stared at a fancy stain on the table, her face pink.

Elder Judith said, 'Meg, why did you bring Callie to see us? We all know what an imaginative girl she is.'

Meg shifted from foot to foot. 'I know it sounds strange, being invisible and talking with animals.' She frowned. 'But what about Tomas? Don't you want to know about Tomas?'

'Yes, we would love to know about Tomas, if it was from a more reliable source,' Elder James said.

Callie's cheeks blazed. She soldiered on. 'Please, there's more. You must hear this, what my good Madach told me.'

Callie waited for Elder James to send them on their way. As he opened his mouth, Elder Judith put her hand on his arm. 'Go on, Callie,' she said kindly. 'We might as well hear the rest.'

Elder James rested the back of his head on the wall, arms folded.

Callie clasped her hands in front of her. Her eyes went from one Elder to the other, then to Meg, whose lips were pressed tight.

'They have machines,' Callie said.

Callie's mind sped back to the Forest, with Tristan. She'd been about to leave when a question had occurred to her.

'Tristan, you said when the wharf was finished the machines would be built. What machines?'

Tristan had hesitated. 'There're two of them, huge machines. At the moment they're in pieces in the holds of the ships.' He'd examined the grass at his feet. 'The engineers need a wide level area to build them. They'll use the wharf when it's done – if they can keep the boar from digging it up.'

'And then?'

Tristan had kept looking at his feet. 'And then,' he said, 'they'll be quick about clearing the forest.'

He'd rushed the rest, apparently wanting to get the worst out as quickly as he could.

'One machine fells the trees, the other one clears and flattens what's left so roads can be built far into the forest, roads which'll take the cutting machine further into the trees, very quickly.'

Callie had no longer seen Tristan, or the Forest around them.

Now, in the inn, with the Elders and Meg frowning at her, the hissing monster of her nightmares towered over her as it had done in the Forest with Tristan ...

... *billowing steam and smoke, its long neck twisting, turning, its gaping, saw-toothed mouth biting the Forest trees, spitting them to the ground ...*

'The trees, the animals, the birds.' Callie's voice was a whisper, her breath caught in her throat. She mustn't close her eyes. If she closed her eyes she would see it all, feel it all.

'Callie?' Meg touched her shoulder. 'What is it?'

'They have machines,' Callie said, her voice flat. 'Monstrous machines, to cut down the trees as quickly as possible.'

She sighed, wriggled to ease the tension from her body.

'They're in pieces in the holds of the ships,' she said. 'The Madach mean to build them soon and when they do, those machines'll destroy the whole Forest. Lord Rafe wants it all.'

Elder James was the first to rouse. He coughed, and said waspishly, 'There can't be such machines. What nonsense, to believe a machine could cut through a whole Forest!' He snorted. 'How could these machines work? Do the Madach have a hundred horses to pull the machines along? I haven't seen any horses.'

'I don't know,' Callie said. 'There's more, though.'

'More?' Elder James turned to Elder Judith. 'Do we have to listen to more?'

Elder Judith's brow wrinkled. She nodded at Callie. 'Go on.'

Callie took a deep breath.

Chapter Twenty Six

Fairytale Slaves

'It's more than trees,' Callie said. 'It's horrible, what the Madach are going to do.'

'More horror?' Elder James sighed heavily. He was clearly fed up with Callie's tales.

Callie didn't notice. She pushed away the nightmare vision … *a fairytale*… and tried to speak calmly.

'They're not going to let us keep our homes and fields once they've finished with the Forest. Captain Jarrow lied.'

Meg's eyebrows drew tight across her forehead. 'Are they going to force us out, like they did from The Place Before?'

Elder James harrumphed. 'If they plan to force us out, why haven't they done it already? If they throw us out, they don't have to worry about guarding us.'

Callie spoke to Meg. 'Do you remember the day the Madach found us and Mr Biggs saying how Captain Jarrow thought we were a fairytale?'

Meg nodded.

'They still think we're a fairytale,' Callie said. 'We are Danae, and the rest of the world has forgotten us.' Her anger rose. 'We're valuable, and they're going to take us with them when they leave. They're going to sell us to Madach lords and ladies like'–she scowled, folding her arms–'like toys, living toys.'

Elder Judith clasped her hands to her chest. 'No, they wouldn't.'

Meg took Callie's hand. Callie could feel her trembling.

Of course. Gwen and Mark! Once people found out they were Danae, they'd be at even more risk from the dangers of the Deep Forest and whatever lay beyond.

Elder James drummed his fingers on the table top. 'I don't believe it for a moment. Why haven't they taken us already? Why wait to cut down trees, why not come back for the trees when there's no one here?'

Elder Judith's fright was apparently eased by her fellow Elder's words.

'Meg, I sympathise with you,' she said, 'given the burdens you've had to bear these past months. However, I see no reason to do anything. We cannot know what Jarrow's real plans are, and the way he's acting suggests he's telling the truth and will leave us in peace when he has what he wants. We have to believe him, Meg.'

Meg put her hand on Callie's shoulder. 'It's true about Captain Jarrow saying we're a fairytale. You were there! You must have heard him.'

The Elders didn't accept or deny this.

'We believe,' Meg said, 'the Madach steal people away. Why not believe they sell them? And it does seem the Madach never see Callie when they're counting us.'

Callie smiled a small smile at these signs of understanding.

'She's a child,' Elder Judith said. 'They might not count the children. Who knows?' She raised her hands, palms up. 'And what about speaking to the wild creatures? And the machine which would cut down a whole forest? Surely those have to be the girl's imagination?'

Meg sighed. 'Yes, the animals.' She squeezed Callie's shoulder. 'Tell the Elders how terrible these Madach truly are. Tell them what your Madach told you about Tomas escaping. Tell them about the village being burned if he does. That's what we came to tell the Elders, isn't it?'

'Burn the village?' Elder Judith whispered.

Elder James rubbed his forehead as if he had a sudden headache.

Elder Judith sighed. 'Callie, I know you have a strong imagination. I know you must miss your brother and sisters. But it's no excuse to cause mischief like this. It could lead to serious trouble.'

'I'm sure you agree,' Elder James said to Elder Judith, 'we shouldn't do anything to upset these Madach. They could yet decide they want our lands, like other Madach did long ago.'

Elder Judith nodded. 'Nothing terrible has happened so far. In fact, you could say Captain Jarrow has been most responsible, watching out for our safety like he has.'

Callie wanted to scream. Nothing terrible? Forced from their homes, locked up in one crowded village, their leader gone! What about not being able to go into the Forest, or being watched over all the time? What about the destruction in the Forest?

Meg squeezed Callie's shoulder again, a warning.

'All's well so far,' Elder Judith said. 'Elder James and I believe it's much safer not to tempt Captain Jarrow into actions we might regret. I'm sure the other Elders and Tomas, if he were here, would agree.'

Callie didn't believe Tomas would agree at all.

Her other thought was how glad she was she hadn't mentioned the dying gryphon, or Child.

***

Meg thanked the Elders for their time and hurried Callie out of the inn.

'That didn't go well, did it?' she said, with a sympathetic smile. 'I don't know what to believe anymore, Callie. Wild creatures and machines, being invisible. What's happening is awful and I know you're desperate to do something. Please remember though, you're one little girl.' Meg gently stroked

138

Callie's hair. 'So this will be an end of it. There is nothing – do you hear me? – nothing you can do in any case. We've told the Elders what you believe, and if anything changes, they've been warned.'

Callie caught the emphasis on 'believe'.

'It's not enough, Ma. Don't you see? The Madach have to be stopped, the machines have to be stopped.'

'But what can I do, what can you do? And what if Captain Jarrow decides we're all too much of a problem?' Meg shuddered. 'Burn the village down. Would we all be in it?'

She hugged Callie. 'You know I can't lose you too, don't you?'

Callie hugged her mother back. She tried to console herself. Maybe it wouldn't be as bad as Tristan said. Maybe he was wrong about the machines, and the fairytale slaves.

No, he wasn't.

***

'Callie, Callie, hush!'

In the moonless night, Meg gathered Callie up, gently waking her from the dreams which had driven her to cry out in her sleep. Meg's cheeks were wet.

Was it Meg or Callie crying?

Soothed by Meg's comforting hold, Callie fell into a dreamless sleep.

Chapter Twenty Seven

An Idea Which Might Work

Callie woke with new purpose.

She smiled as her mother watched her anxiously over breakfast. She ate her bread and cheese and drank her milk, slowly, no gulping it down. Her mother returned Callie's smile and went upstairs to gather a pile of mending.

Callie darted out of the cottage and down to the gate.

Yes! She was in time.

The working Danae were almost all through. Callie slipped in close behind the last villager and out through the gate. None of the Madach nor the Danae noticed. She could see Peter and his father further down the track, heading to the mill.

Callie ran into the Forest, threading fast around trees and ferns and bushes. She took the long way around to avoid the Madach tracks and the scorched swathes of what had once been Forest, steering clear of places where Madach might be moving about, to where the rabbit had found Tristan before.

He was there, sitting under an ash tree in the fresh morning air, scribbling in his leather notebook.

***

Tristan's mind had whirled with indecision over the past days.

He didn't want to back out of his promise to Callie. He was certain he was doing the right thing helping the Danae. What troubled him, deeply, was how Jarrow would punish Callie and the villagers. He'd had no sleep with Jarrow's bullying threats tumbling around his skull like acrobats in a circus. He wasn't worried for himself, at least not about Jarrow. The worst Jarrow could do would be to lock Tristan in his cabin all the way back to Etting. He also wasn't afraid of how his father might punish him. Well, not too afraid.

No. What caused Tristan anguish in the sleepless hours of the night was the certainty of his father's bitter disappointment at being let down by Tristan, again.

He watched Callie approach, seeing the determination in her face. He sighed. He wished he could be that sure of things.

'Hello, Callie? What did the Elders say?'

Callie flopped down beside Tristan, panting from her race through the Forest. She rubbed her shoulders against the smooth trunk of the ash and wrinkled her nose.

'They don't want to know or do anything. They believe your Captain Jarrow will do what he's promised and leave when he has his timber.'

A sharp prick of guilty relief eased Tristan's confusion. He wouldn't have to choose.

Callie twisted to face him. Tristan had to look away from her intent gaze.

'Last night, I was going over and over it, and it seems to me'–Callie clapped her hands–'if the machines are in pieces, we should get rid of some of the pieces so the machines won't work.'

We?

Tristan's relief was short-lived.

He tried a sensible argument.

'Not sure that'd work,' he said. 'They'll have plenty of spare parts. Stealing a few bits might delay things but I think it'd be impossible to really stop the machines.'

Callie squinted at him in the bright sunlight nudging its way through the branches. 'So we have to steal lots and lots of pieces.'

Yes. Lots and lots. And lots.

That was the only way to stop the machines. If it could be done. If Tristan was brave enough.

'Tristan?'

Callie's green eyes found Tristan's brown ones. The eyes belonging to a girl from a conquered people, soon to be dragged off over the oceans and sold as a fairytale slave. He saw again Alfred's feet slipping on the icy grass, heard the cut off cry.

Tristan slowly scratched his cheek. 'If whole crates of pieces went missing, somehow,' he said at last, 'that would make the machines unworkable.'

Callie grinned. 'Of course! The Forest creatures'll help us.'

Us?

'The forest creatures?' Tristan said aloud.

'Yes, you'll see. We can do it.'

It was like being dragged along by a swollen river to the edge of a thunderous waterfall.

Tristan tried to keep his head above water.

'You do understand, don't you,' he said, 'that it'll be pretty impossible to do, that failure is very likely, and worse, if it does work, it'll look deliberate? Jarrow'll blame the Danae. He'll come up with some dreadful punishment.'

Like burning villages. For a start.

Callie drew in a long breath. 'Do we have a choice?' She touched Tristan's arm. 'And if you're caught, you'll be in trouble too, won't you?'

Trouble?

Do the right thing? Be assured of his father's disappointed fury?

Tristan balanced the two on an imaginary scales.

'Yes. I'll be in a heap of trouble.'

He laughed, a part-relieved and part-desperate high giggle – and plunged head down, arms and legs thrashing, over the thunderous waterfall.

Callie laughed too.

'But,' Tristan said when he was calmer, 'how by the Beings are we going to get rid of whole crates of heavy machinery?'

'Come on,' Callie said. 'Let me show you our wild army.'

***

Tristan and Callie perched on the old willow's snarled roots while the rabbit summoned the wild creatures. Callie's thoughts went to Gwen and Mark, out there in the Deep Forest. Perhaps they'd found the Sleih by now, and Lucy.

'Tristan?'

'Yes?'

'Do you know if the Sleih are real?'

'The Sleih?' Tristan's brow furrowed. 'Assumed they were a fairytale. On the other hand, I thought the Danae were a fairytale, so who knows?'

'Doesn't help much.'

'Why do you want to know?'

Callie told Tristan about Lucy disappearing, and how Meg was sure she must be with the Sleih because of the hoof prints which went west. She told him too the legend about the Sleih once helping the Danae, and Gwen and Mark fleeing into the Forest in search of these mythical people to beg for an army to fight the Madach.

At the end, Tristan said, 'Let's hope they find them and let's hope your sister's there and let's hope the Sleih send an army to save you all.'

Callie sighed. 'Such a lot of hoping.'

She leaned forward on the root, staring past Tristan and beyond the hanging branches of the willow.

Callie never found out what the rabbit told the other creatures. Whatever it was, they came, shyly, eyeing the stranger.

'Here's the army we do have,' she said softly, 'even if it's not as powerful as the Sleih.'

Chapter Twenty Eight

Unexpected Help

The Danae working group approached the gate to the village, Madach before and after them.

'Don't look down.'

Peter jumped at Callie's whispered instruction. He didn't look down. At least, not until they were all through the gate and heading for the roundup in the square.

While the Danae milled about waiting to be counted, Peter said, 'You frightened me.'

Callie grinned.

'What's going on, Callie? Did your mother know you were out today?'

'No, her mother did not.' Meg stood beside them, no tears this time. 'Are you in this too, Peter?'

'In what?'

There was no time for more. The counting had begun and the square fell quiet, each line of Danae dawdling back to their homes once done. Peter was sure the Madach counted over Callie's head. Afterwards, he watched Meg haul Callie home. Which didn't stop Callie from waving at him, still grinning as she went.

Something was going on. Peter frowned after her, half-waved back.

***

'I worry, Callie. Can't you see how much I worry?'

Meg and Callie sat on the bench beside the cottage wall. Callie hadn't received a scolding. Instead, Meg had been sad. 'Don't you see? I have enough to worry about with Lucy, Gwen and Mark?'

'I'm sorry, Ma. It's just, well, no one's doing anything to save us.'

Meg managed a tired smile. 'So, assuming we need saving, it has to be you, does it?'

'It's in my dreams.'

Ginger Cat's soft warm fur coiled about Callie's bare legs. She reached down to pat him.

'In your dreams?'

'My nightmares. You know, when I wake up, crying?' Callie's voice fell. 'The monster, the huge monster, hissing and steaming, smoke everywhere ...' She stopped. She didn't dare close her eyes. She looked at Meg instead. 'The monster is real, Ma, it's here. The Madach have brought it here.'

Meg sighed. 'Callie, those are nightmares, and it's terrible you have nightmares, but it doesn't mean they'll come true.'

Callie stared at a pot of geraniums silhouetted in the moonlight against the whitewashed wall opposite.

The nightmares *would* come true if those machines weren't stopped, she wanted to say. She wanted to tell Meg about Tristan and the wild army and how they planned to stop the machines. Would she understand? Probably not. Worse, she could make it impossible for Callie to leave the village.

A few people strolled in the narrow lanes, tempted out by the mild air for a walk or to visit neighbours or the inn, which buzzed every night with arguments about the problem of the Madach.

Beyond the wooden fence, a fox cried out.

Meg gave Callie a strong hug. 'I'm not happy, not at all,' she murmured into Callie's dark curls. 'Remember what I said. No more nonsense, please. I can't lose you as well.'

Callie didn't say anything. She watched Meg walk inside. Ginger Cat stalked ahead, head and tail up, like a herald announcing a queen.

'How upset is she?'

Callie hadn't seen Peter approach along the dusty lane. She tapped the bench to invite him to sit down. Ignoring his question, she asked one of her own.

'Don't you think, Peter, we Danae should be doing more to protect ourselves from these Madach?'

Peter snorted. 'More? Anything would be good. This is all wrong.' He waved his hands. 'It's not just about being locked up. It's also about not knowing what those Madach are doing out there in our Forest and,' he lowered his voice although there was no one to hear, 'what they're going to do with us. They can't leave us like this forever, can they?'

Callie didn't answer. At least, not out loud.

Peter shrugged. 'Since Tomas went, the Elders haven't done anything, or even spoken to us. Who knows what they're thinking?'

'I do,' Callie said. 'Do you want to know?'

'You know? How? Tell me.'

Callie told Peter everything she'd said to the Elders. She told him how Elders Judith and James refused to believe her. She told him about the desolation spreading like a disease through the Forest at the hands of the Madach. She watched his face whiten at the pictures she painted. She finished by telling him about Tristan, and the wild creatures, and how they were going to destroy the monstrous machines.

Peter ran his hands through his pale yellow hair. 'Ahh,' he said. 'I can see why the Elders had trouble believing you. It's a lot to take in.'

Callie stared again at the geraniums. Peter didn't believe her either.

'They're right you know, about the risk,' Peter said. 'If you and this Madach upset Captain Jarrow, the Danae will suffer.'

Callie started up from the bench to go inside. She was angry with herself for thinking Peter might believe her, and sad there was no one she could trust. Except Tristan, her supposed enemy.

But Peter put his hand on her arm. 'Slaves, eh?' he said. 'They want to sell us as fairytale slaves?'

He drew a deep breath, sighed it out. His eyes didn't leave Callie's face.

'I've seen you come and go without the Madach noticing. Which makes me tend to believe you, although meetings with boar and foxes, hmm…'

He rubbed his hand across his forehead as if his head was hurting from the tumult of thoughts racing there.

'This isn't a game. You know that, don't you, Callie? You do know the Forest, and us, and the animals too, are all in danger from these Madach and we have to find a way to make them leave?'

Callie slumped back onto the bench.

'Oh yes, I know,' she said. 'It's what I've been trying to tell everyone. Dreadful, dreadful things are going to happen. More than what they're doing already.' Callie's hands clutched the edge of the bench. 'I saw it, in my mind, the first day they arrived. Even before, I saw it in my dreams, awful dreams. It's what I've been trying to tell Ma, about my dreams. The monster cutting through the trees, the Forest bare, full of ragged stumps, the animals dying.' She fixed her sea-green eyes on Peter's face. 'I've seen us, the Danae, in a strange market place. Our clothes are ragged. We're hungry. There are Madach with whips.'

Callie flicked the tears from her eyes. 'Yes, Peter, I know it's not a game.'

Peter looked up at the moon-bright sky.

'Do you and this Tristan and'–he paused, shaking his head–

'the boar and the foxes and the rest of them, need help with this plan of yours?'

Callie's tears dried. She beamed. 'Yes please!'

Chapter Twenty Nine

Friends

Sheets of rain driven by cold, keening winds kept everyone huddled inside. The Danae with livestock to care for were the only ones to venture through the gate, they and their Madach escorts glumly hunched under sodden cloaks.

Callie had to stay in the house. She helped with chores and when they were done she read a book she found in her temporary home. It was an old book of fairytales and there was a story about a wicked Sleih king who stole all the children and their parents could never find them no matter where they searched.

Another story said that once upon a very long time ago, the mythical Sleih lived in caverns in the mountains and learned magic from gryphons. Callie wondered at the picture of the gryphon. It was Child, grownup.

If gryphons were real ... what did that mean about the Sleih ...? Callie's heart beat faster.

***

The sun shone. The village lanes, softened to muddy wallows by the unrelenting rain, sparkled in the morning light. Danae farmers squelched between the cottages to gather at the gate, anxious to discover what damage the storm had wrought.

Callie stuck close to Peter, and they were out. She ducked into the surrounding trees and ran.

Tristan wasn't under the ash, so Callie went to the willow. It wasn't long before the rabbit appeared.

Is it today?

'No,' Callie said. 'I need to find Tristan to tell him something important. But, have you seen Child?'

The rabbit's ears fell back. *No.*

'I'm worried about him. After all, he's only a baby, isn't he?'

The rabbit didn't appear to believe Child needed to be worried about.

Callie was insistent. 'Can we go to the cave, see if he's there? I need your help. I can't find it by myself.'

The rabbit twitched its nose, waggled its ears and slowly, very slowly hopped through the trees.

They made their way along the ridge, the sun getting higher, although little of its light filtered through the leaves. It was hot under the airless canopy and Callie was soon damp with sweat. She was grateful when they reached the grassy bowl sooner than she expected. There it was, the white mist hiding its colourful secrets. This time Callie led the way down the slope, the rabbit following. A quiet stillness soothed her as she threaded through the dancing birds and butterflies and the vivid flowers – different flowers, as though the grassy bowl found it amusing to conform to the seasons above the mist.

There was no sign of Child. They reached the cave. Callie pushed aside the vines – covered now in tiny yellow flowers where bees busied themselves – which straggled over the crumbling arch. She peeked through, remembering too late about the dead gryphon, and breathed out in relief when there was no sign of bones or feathers.

Muted light fell from the hole in the rocky roof. Child lay under the light, his tail curled around him, his tawny sides gently rising up and down.

The rabbit stayed close to Callie as she gazed at the sleeping creature.

'He's grown a lot,' she said softly. She didn't dare make jokes about eating things. 'Let's go outside and wait for him to wake up. Best not to startle him, hey?'

The rabbit had scampered out through the flowered curtain before Callie finished her sentence.

Callie drank the sweet water from the pool and rested beside the yellow stones, watching the birds flying between the trees. It was peaceful in the grassy bowl. The crowded village, the hissing monster, the destructive Madach, were far away.

The rabbit crouched at her feet, facing the entrance to the cave with unblinking eyes. Callie felt its sudden jump against her leg.

Strings of the yellow-flowered curtain tossed wildly in the air.

A blue, feathered head with a sharply curved beak hurtled through, followed by a long length of tawny lion body. Child pranced up to Callie, danced in front of her. He waggled his head from side to side, fixing her with first one, then the other, deep green eye, on a level with her own.

The beak opened. Callie smiled back.

Child bent his head to the round-eyed rabbit, nudging it with his beak before flying off, sweeping low and fast around the grassy bowl.

Showing off, Callie realised. He was pleased to see them.

The rabbit trembled against Callie's foot.

'He won't harm you.' Callie squatted down to stroke the brown fur. 'He's playing, like a big friendly dog.'

The rabbit rolled its eyes. *Yes, and rabbits get on fine with dogs, don't they?*

Callie giggled. Nevertheless, she kept one hand on the rabbit when Child skidded to a stop in front of them. His talons left long scars in the grass. He flopped in front of Callie and blinked up at her.

The rabbit backed away.

151

Callie stroked the feathers on Child's head. He rolled over, offering his tummy to be scratched. She obliged, laughing.

'You poor thing, have you been lonely?'

The deep green eyes were solemn. Child wriggled onto his stomach to face the rabbit, hunched by the pool.

Slowly, Child crawled toward the glassy-eyed rabbit. Callie watched. She was mostly sure this would be all right.

When Child was near, he rolled on his back, stuck his legs straight up in the air and closed his eyes, playing dead.

Funny, isn't he? The rabbit relaxed, a bit.

Callie giggled again. 'Oh,' she said.

The rabbit had hopped on to Child's exposed tummy and kneaded the white fur, scratching him as Callie had.

Child's body squirmed along the ground. The rabbit leaped off. Its chest rose and fell and its mouth opened in surprise at its own bravery.

Child rolled onto his front and stretched his neck to brush his blue head against the rabbit's much much smaller brown one. The rabbit's heart slowed to a normal beat.

It seemed the rabbit and the baby gryphon were friends.

***

The grassy bowl had grown warmer by the time Callie decided she should climb through the mist to head back to the Forest. The rabbit promised to return with playmates for the boisterous baby gryphon. Callie knew it had young boar in mind, or a few sturdy badgers.

Child watched them leave with hooded eyes, tail curled between his back legs.

'Don't be sad,' Callie said. Her heart twisted as she waved good-bye. 'We'll be back soon, I promise.'

She and the rabbit reached the ridge and Callie paused to gaze back down into what was now a normal forest of trees and bushes.

The rabbit had hopped ahead, along the top of the ridge.

Callie shrugged and went after the rabbit, pushing her way down through bracken and ferns in search of Tristan. As they came closer to the sea, the rabbit led her onto one of the Madach's new, wide tracks. Callie wasn't sure this was a good idea. There were too many Madach about, inspecting their own storm damage – heavy branches across the track, fences down, a vegetable plot full of muddy holes.

Not all caused by the storm, Callie decided, cheered by the thought.

Callie and the rabbit had to jump into the trees several times and Callie's nerves were stretched tight when, at last, the rabbit left the track to lead her further into the Forest. She followed its white tail, bobbing around brambles and low bushes, to a clearing filled with pink and white foxgloves. Tristan was here, head tilted back, staring up at a tall pine.

Callie coughed.

Tristan spun around, dropping his notebook.

'Callie! Why are you here? How did you find me?'

She pointed to the rabbit, resting on its back legs, clearly saying, *Good thing one of us knows our way around this Forest.*

'I had to come and see you today. There's someone who wants to help us.'

'Good,' Tristan said, when Callie had told him about Peter. 'Any help is good.'

The rabbit was given new instructions, concentrating on Callie's face all the time.

Callie saw Tristan trying not to laugh.

'What's funny?'

'You and the rabbit, you're both so serious.'

The rabbit flicked its ears. *Of course we're serious. We play with gryphons.*

Chapter Thirty

Captain Jarrow Is Upset

'Roast haunch of venison, that's what my stomach wants.' Captain Jarrow chewed his skinny chicken leg with a disgruntled sneer. He tossed the gnawed bone onto his greasy plate and tipped back his chair.

'Where do you think they've all gone, hey, Sir Tristan? Answer me that! Where have all the deer gone, hey?'

Tristan flinched at Captain Jarrow's bark. His mind had also been on deer, only not to eat them. As it had been on boar and foxes and weasels and all the creatures in Callie's wild army. His stomach constantly twitched with nerves – at the risk they were all taking, at his own daring, at the constant worry about what Captain Jarrow's revenge would be if Callie and her army succeeded.

And what would happen if they failed.

'Deer, Captain?' Tristan said. 'Gone?'

'Yes, Sir Tristan. Gone, disappeared, run away over the hill and far away.' Captain Jarrow's black eyebrows beetled. 'Along with the rabbits and anything else edible in this damn forest.'

'Not the boar, Captain,' one of the lieutenants dared say.

Captain Jarrow's scowl deepened. 'As you point out, Lieutenant, not the boar.'

The table of men fell silent.

Clive, the chief engineer, shrunk lower in his seat and concentrated on chewing his last boiled potato.

It didn't help.

'By the Beings! How long does it take to build a simple fence, hey?' Captain Jarrow's bark found Clive.

Clive reluctantly raised his eyes from his plate. 'Not long, Captain, if the timber to build it stayed where it was put.'

Tristan hid his grin behind his serviette. Poor Clive.

Captain Jarrow had decided to fix the boar's nightly digging up of the earth-packed wharf by building a fence around it. One strong enough, with posts dug deep enough, to resist tusks and snouts. Each day new posts for the fence were cut and shaped and given pointed ends top and bottom. Each evening they were laid in tidy piles where they were to be erected, and each morning the tidy piles were scattered across the wharf and in among the bushes. Many went missing altogether and Tristan, along with everyone else, suspected they were at the bottom of the sea.

After the third night, Clive's engineers tied thick rope around bundles of the posts. The rope was chewed through, in more than one place, and tangled into a knotted, useless mess. The sailors complained, as it was their rope and they needed it for the ships if they were to sail safely back to Etting.

Now, on this fourth night, Captain Jarrow had ordered guards set, with strung bows and arrows ready. It had worsened his already foul temper.

'Not enough men,' he'd complained long and loudly to Tristan who happened to be around when the order was given.

(Luckily. As it was lucky Callie had later found Tristan in the forest and he could warn her and the rabbit who in turn would warn the boar and the badgers.)

'Have to guard the Danae, now have to guard the fence,' Captain Jarrow said, jabbing his fork into the remains of the stringy chicken. 'Told your noble father I needed more soldiers, didn't I, hey Sir Tristan?'

Tristan said yes, Captain Jarrow had indeed. And not said,

Thank the Beings Father didn't go along with needing more soldiers.

'Is it Danae getting out at night?' another lieutenant at the table said. 'Is it them doing the damage?'

Captain Jarrow glared. 'If it is, it'll be your men's necks on the line.'

The lieutenant blanched. 'No, it can't be, not with all the patrolling we do as well as keeping watch at the gate.'

'No,' Captain Jarrow said. 'It can't be.'

He tugged hard at his beard, loosening tiny bits of chicken which had stuck there.

'It's those damnable boar,' he said. He thumped his ham fist on the table so hard the cutlery clattered. 'And if I can't have roast venison for my dinner, then I want roast boar! Hear me?'

The lieutenants heard him. As did the rest of the ship.

Tristan's anxiety about his and Callie's plan fermented in his stomach like curdled milk.

Chapter Thirty One

The Signal

They waited.

They waited while the Madach finished building the sturdy fence around the wharf, stopping the boar's nightly raids. They waited while the Madach repaired the damaged surface, making sure all was level. When the surface was ready, the Madach at last began to bring up the crates and boxes which held the pieces of the machines.

By the middle of the second afternoon, there was a long neat row of crates and boxes lined up on the wharf. A number were open, and a few big parts lay on canvas sheets beneath a temporary shelter.

Tristan strolled into the forest, taking his notebook with him. And as it did every day, Callie's rabbit soon found him. It rested on its back legs and peered up at him, one ear down.

'Tonight,' Tristan said. He found it strange to talk to a rabbit. 'Let Callie know it's tonight.'

The rabbit loped off to the Danae village.

***

Callie sat on the grass with her back to the palings of the tall fence, her legs stuck out in front. The book on her lap stayed open at the same page. It was no good, she couldn't take in the meaning of the words. Not with her eyes forever going to the small hole under the fence – one end of a tunnel the rabbits had dug from the edge of the Forest.

She closed the book, tilting her head back to rest on the fence. The excitement of doing something was wearing thin with the waiting.

Every day, Peter wanted to know, 'Will it be tomorrow?' or 'What's taking so long?' or 'Does this Tristan truly mean to help us?'

Every day, Callie had to say, 'I've no idea,' in response to the first two questions. As for the last, Callie kept faith in her Madach friend, while wishing something would happen soon.

Callie knew Meg kept a close eye on her and was pleased Callie was no longer slipping out of the village. Meg seemed to assume Callie had given up on her idea of saving the Danae. Sometimes, when the two of them were working about the house, helping Jethro's mother with the cooking or the cleaning or in the garden, Callie would want to tell Meg everything.

She held back because she was afraid Meg wouldn't understand. It would make her worry even more.

Callie's conscience challenged her – should you be plotting like this?

Her thoughts went back and forth, weighing up Captain Jarrow's certain revenge against the horrors of her nightmares. At any time, day or night, the hissing monster would creep from the shadows of her mind… *biting at the Forest trees… the animals fleeing ... their fear searing her mind ...*

The choice was made.

A twitching nose wriggled in the small hole. Callie jumped. She glanced around. All was clear.

'Tonight?' she said to the rabbit.

The pink nose twitched some more. Seeing no one nearby, the rabbit dared to come out of the tunnel. It crept close to Callie. *Yes, yes, tonight, the tall one says tonight.*

'Yes!' Callie said softly. 'Now you need to go down to the mill and find Peter, like we planned.'

She stood up, grabbing at the book to save it falling to the ground. 'I'll see you and Peter later, at the willow tree.'

The rabbit scampered back into the tunnel with a flash of white tail.

Callie tried not to run all the way to her friend Suzie's house. Someone might want to know what she was excited about.

***

Peter hefted the grain from the store, throwing the rough sacks over his shoulder and laying them by the wide door of the mill. Nearby, the great wheel turned in its long, noisy arc, the mill race bubbling and frothing, sending out fine sprays of water.

Through the spray, Peter caught sight of a rabbit hunched next to the glistening wet stones. The rabbit didn't run off when it saw Peter watching. It rose up on its back legs and twitched its nose.

This must be the signal Callie had told him to expect.

'Tonight?' Peter felt foolish talking to a rabbit.

The rabbit hopped closer, keeping its eyes on Peter's face. The nose kept twitching.

This had to be Callie's rabbit.

The miller bustled out of the mill door, eyeing the pile of grain sacks. The rabbit bolted into the hedge.

'Need help, son?'

'Thanks, Dad.'

A nervous fear settled in the base of Peter's stomach. Tonight, at last. By the Beings, he hoped it worked.

***

Tristan gathered cheese and bread from the galley into a sack, grabbed a bottle or two of the ship's weak beer and wandered back into the Forest.

No one took any notice. They all knew Sir Tristan was always wandering into the Forest, supposedly counting trees which the woodsmen would later cut down.

***

Peter strode up the track to the village, no time to stroll and enjoy the mild evening tonight. He was soon ahead of his father, not quite up to the farmers walking ahead. At a curve in the track where high summer grasses meant he could be seen neither from behind nor from the gate, he stopped, glanced all around, and plunged into the trees.

He waited for a Madach voice to demand to know what he was doing.

Peter squatted behind a chestnut tree and peeked around its trunk. His father and the last of the Danae passed by with their Madach escort.

***

The miller came through the gate. He was tired from his day's work of shifting bulging sacks and eager to get home for supper and, later, a pint of ale in the inn.

He wasn't worried by Peter's absence. He assumed his son was ahead of him, heading for the square and the evening roundup.

Chapter Thirty Two

An Escape

Callie stood in the square, not far from her mother. Her shoulders were back, her chin jutted out.

The Danae behind them had been counted and were heading to their suppers. Callie kept her eyes on the Madach counting her row. His finger went up and down as he checked off each villager in turn.

He came to Callie. She wriggled, coughed.

'You can see me,' she mumbled softly.

Her mother frowned across at her.

The Madach pointed his finger at Callie's dark curls, check! He moved on to the next Danae.

The roundup was complete, the tally correct.

***

Callie walked back to the cottage beside Meg.

As they reached the door, Callie took Meg's hand and led her to the bench beside the wall. The evening summer sun shone redly on the pot of geraniums.

'What's going on, Callie?'

Callie didn't hesitate. 'We have a plan,' she said, 'me and Tristan and Peter. And the wild creatures. We're going to destroy those machines I told you about.' She kept her eyes on the geraniums. 'It's tonight. Peter's already in the Forest. It's why I had to be counted in the roundup, instead of him.'

Meg gasped.

'It's too dangerous.' Her voice trembled. 'What if you're caught? What if you're hurt? The Madach have weapons, they're stronger than us.'

'Yes, perhaps, but ...'

'You're just a little girl,' Meg said, 'and Peter's not much more than a boy.'

Callie set her heart against Meg's pleading.

'I have to go, Ma, don't you see? I have to make sure the wild creatures know what to do. Nobody else can do that. Only me.'

Meg sniffed. 'Wild creatures! By the Beings, Callie, you're far too old for this kind of make-believe. Talking to creatures, indeed.'

Callie chose another way. 'This is about saving the Danae and saving the Forest. You can't not let me go. It's too, too important.'

Meg picked angrily at the folds of her skirt. 'You're determined to do this, aren't you?'

'No one else is doing anything.'

Meg left off picking at her skirt and sighed. 'I know. I know, Callie.' Her voice became petulant. 'It's bad enough Lucy and your Da being taken. Then Gwen and Mark, now you. Why is it me who has to sacrifice my children?'

An early owl hooted in the trees beyond the tall fence. Closer by, the smell of suppers cooking tickled Callie's nose. She waited.

'It appears I'm destined to be the mother of heroes,' Meg said, a catch in her voice.

Callie looked at her. A rueful smile played on Meg's lips.

'It's your Da. You all get your courage from your Da.' Meg's eyes glistened. 'Have to do something special, be braver than the rest.'

She stroked Callie's hand. 'It's why he chose to be a

fisherman, because everybody else said it was too dangerous. He loved it, out there on the ocean in all weathers. Said it made him know he was truly alive. Said coming home was all the sweeter for the danger of it.' Meg sniffed. 'He taught me courage too, learning to wait, be patient, have confidence he would always come home.'

Callie blinked through her own tears.

'And one day he didn't come home,' Meg said, so softly Callie had to strain to hear. 'Then Lucy, and, well, my courage fled.'

Callie threw her arms around Meg's neck. 'I'm sorry, Ma. Can you find just a bit more courage, please? Because I have to do this.'

Silence, for a long while.

'Of course you do. I know that.' Meg gently pulled Callie's arms away and leaned back to smile at her. 'It will be all right, my girl, it will be all right. And if it's not, I'll have a lot to say to those craven Elders.'

Callie laughed, hiccoughed. Meg laughed too, the sound a little high.

'How are you going to get out of the village?' she said.

'Don't worry. Already organised.'

***

Sometime after supper, a noisy gang of children made their way to the gate in the fence. It was too light for bed, so here they were, kicking and throwing a colourful ball to each other.

As they neared the gate, a boy kicked the ball way up in the air. The children froze, watching it clear the wooden fence.

The children noisily berated the boy who had kicked the ball.

'I'll get it for you.' The guard on the other side of the fence called out.

But Callie's friend Suzie shouted, 'Don't touch it!'

She curled her small fingers around a fence paling, laughing face pressed to the slender gap. 'If you pick it up, because you're a boy, the boys will have won. Please don't touch it!'

Callie watched from her place next to the gate, admiring, as Suzie cajoled the guard to join in the spirit of the game.

'What do you want me to do?' he said, gruffly.

'Couldn't you please open the gate for a second and let me go get it?'

Callie hoped the guard had children of his own, back home. It appeared he did. Grumbling loudly about it being only one little girl, after all, he opened the gate.

It wasn't one little girl, though. All the children piled through, jostling each other out of the way, pushing and shoving, coming close to knocking the guard down as they scrambled to be the first to pick up the ball.

'Hey, hey, hey!' The guard shooed them back inside where they ran off into the square, noisily chasing the boy who had won the ball.

Suzie stopped to look back. She waved, and the guard raised his eyebrows in an exasperated manner and gave a quick wave in return.

A short way behind him, on the edge of the Forest, Callie also waved at her friend. Then she ran through the trees, up and over the ridge, to the old willow tree.

Chapter Thirty Three

Peter And Tristan

Peter watched the last of the Danae and the Madach pass by along the track to the village. He waited and watched a while longer before stepping out of the trees. The quiet emptiness did nothing to soothe the nervous fear which had settled in the base of his stomach. He hurried back to the mill.

The rabbit waited there, grooming its long ears, barely out of reach of the spray from the creaking wheel. It twitched its nose at Peter, peering into his eyes.

Did it think Peter could hear it, like Callie supposedly could?

No matter how hard Peter peered back, no rabbit-like thoughts came to him.

The rabbit dropped its gaze and hopped slowly along by the side of the hedge. It stood on its back legs, twitched its nose some more, and dropped to the ground to go on its way.

Callie had said the rabbit would lead Peter to an old willow where he would meet Tristan. Peter followed the rabbit.

They skirted past the larger, empty village and down into the Forest, using hardly seen animal paths and hurrying through open grassy areas where pink and white foxgloves were in full bloom. Despite the bright summer evening, it was shadowy and cool beneath the trees. The knot in Peter's stomach loosened the further they came from the village and any chance of stumbling into stray Madach. It had been a long time since he'd wandered among the trees. He hadn't realised how much he'd missed the peace of their mid-summer stillness.

Head down to concentrate on the way forward, Peter nearly trod on the rabbit when it abruptly stopped at a curtain of willow branches. With a blink at Peter, the rabbit disappeared into the willow's depths.

Peter bent down to peek inside.

'Oh!'

He hadn't been at all sure about the existence of Callie's so-called good Madach. There he was, however – perched on a thick tree root, his back against the willow's rough trunk.

But what had made Peter gasp was the sight of Callie's wild army, exactly as she'd claimed. Boar, badgers, rabbits and foxes surrounded the young Madach. A gentle hooting made Peter jump. Two owls rested in the willow's branches.

Were they coming along too?

Peter waited outside the willow's shelter while the Madach picked his way between the sleeping animals and scrambled out from under the tree's branches.

They faced each other, Tristan head and shoulders taller than Peter, both otherwise of a similar, slim build.

'You must be Callie's good Madach.' Peter held his hand out, remembering. He'd seen this young Madach before, when Captain Jarrow first came to the village.

Tristan grasped the offered hand, laughing. 'Yes, that's what she calls me. I'm Tristan. And you're Peter.'

'We're very grateful…' Peter began at the same time Tristan said, 'I was worried about Callie doing this alone…'

There was a silence, which allowed both of them to hear Peter's stomach rumble. He blushed.

Tristan gestured to the inside of the willow. 'Can I offer you supper while we wait?'

They waited within the willow's shelter, munching their way through the bread and cheese from the ship, washed down by the weak ale. Peter kept stealing looks at Tristan. He recalled the first Danae encounter with the Madach and how he'd wondered at the time whom the finely dressed young man might be. Seeing Tristan's smooth hands now, he knew he was no labourer or sailor.

He propped the mug of ale against a tree root. 'What's your part in this expedition, Tristan?'

Tristan shrugged. 'I count the trees, the different types, and write reports for Captain Jarrow, a sort of clerk I suppose.'

'Hmm.' Peter knew what a clerk was. There was one in the villages whom you could go to if you needed a letter done about some business matter and weren't sure of the right words to use. 'You're better dressed than our clerk,' he said, 'like you come from a well-off family.'

Tristan's face reddened.

Peter had a startling thought. He thought of something Callie had said, in passing, when she told him about the plan. 'The other Madach call him Sir Tristan, although he likes to be called Tristan.'

Peter faced Tristan squarely. 'Callie said the other Madach call you Sir Tristan. Are you,' he paused, 'of a noble family?'

Tristan's blush grew deeper, although he held Peter's gaze.

'You're not, are you, related to this Lord Rafe whom Captain Jarrow goes on about?'

'I'm his son.' Tristan straightened his shoulders. 'Trouble is, he doesn't like me much. I'm a disappointment because I'm not enthusiastic about conquering people and building manufactories.'

Peter frowned.

***

'Oh, good, you found each other.'

Callie pushed aside the curtain of willow branches, breathless from running. The rabbit hopped to her side and she bent to brush its silky ears.

Peter looked up at her, Tristan stood. Neither greeted her.

'What's wrong? What's happened?' Callie frowned between gasps. 'Have they put guards on the wharf again?'

'Callie,' Peter said, 'do you know who Tristan is?'

Callie's frown deepened. 'Yes, he's a good Madach who's helping us.'

Peter pursed his lips. 'He also happens to be Lord Rafe's son.'

'Lord Rafe's son? The greedy Lord Rafe who wants our Forest? And he's going to help us?' Callie beamed. 'Thank you, Tristan.'

Peter rolled his eyes.

Tristan said, 'Peter's worried I'll betray you.'

Callie's hands went to her hips. 'Why?' she said to Peter. 'Can't Tristan have his own feelings about things? It's hard enough for him to disobey awful Captain Jarrow, yet he's doing it.'

She glared at Peter, her green eyes glinting. He glared back.

Callie waved her hand at the resting creatures. 'I know Tristan won't betray us. The animals wouldn't have come if he was planning on betraying us.'

The rabbit hopped from Callie to Tristan, rose on its back legs and twitched its nose at him. Tristan leaned down to stroke the soft brown head.

'I'm supposed to be all right about this because a *rabbit* says I should?' Peter said.

'Yes. It's the best recommendation anyone can have.'

'Then I guess I have to go with it. However,' Peter's eyes locked with Tristan's, 'if the rabbit turns out to be a bad judge of character, you'll know all about it.'

Tristan rose to his full height. 'You won't be sorry, I promise.'

A boar grunted in its sleep.

Callie beamed. 'Good. When can we go?'

Chapter Thirty Four

Destruction

They waited, an awkwardness between Tristan and Peter.

Callie ignored it. She bounced up and down, her excitement passing like a contagion to the gathered creatures. There was a lot of snuffling and grunting and pawing and flapping. They'd all had enough rest and were as keen as Callie to get on with the night's work.

The evening darkened. The moon was a thin white glow on the horizon. It was time to leave.

The rabbit wouldn't be going with them. Callie had begged it to stay behind, pleading that a battle in the dark was no place for a rabbit. It had sulked and hopped away from the willow, towards the ridge.

The young people and the Forest creatures made their cautious way down to the Madach ships. The Forest was quiet around them, as though the trees were holding their breath.

They reached the heavy fence around the wharf. Peter, Callie and the boar crept to the end furthest from the ships. Tristan went to the narrow gate, slid the bolt, gave Callie and Peter a 'good luck' thumbs up and headed to the ship. He left the gate open. As he crossed the gangplank, he picked up the heavy chain lying coiled on one side. The chain rattled. He held it for a moment before slowly stretching it across the opening and winding the end tightly over the ship's railing.

The badgers ambled over to two of the wooden posts in

the fence, not far apart, and at the furthest corner from the gangplank. The badgers had been busy tunnelling under and around these posts for the last several nights.

Two giant sows nudged at the fence between the posts. It wobbled and they lifted their big heads up and down, approving the badgers' work. Other boar joined them. Peter and Callie each stood by one of the two weak posts, ready to help.

The owls flew low overhead. They hooted softly. All was clear.

'Let's push,' Callie whispered to the boar.

They pushed, Peter and Callie, the boar, all together. The badgers had worked hard. Both posts quickly gave way, the lengths of planking between them falling to the ground with a soft thwack which made Callie glance nervously at the ships.

No movement there.

The boar trotted, without grunts and snorts, to the crates and boxes which had been brought up from the ships' holds.

In the darkness, Callie couldn't tell which crates were already partly unpacked and which were closed. She trusted the boar to remember Tristan's instruction to 'Go for the open ones first.'

The boar reached the crates. Callie's breath caught in her throat.

The nightmare loomed ... *the hissing monster marching through the Forest, ripping the trees from the earth, spitting them to the ground.*

Callie wanted to race in with the boar. She wanted to heave those innocent-looking crates into the water herself and destroy the monsters inside.

She grabbed the fence tightly. She mustn't go in. She'd be in the way.

She watched, fidgeting, her heart pounding.

Strong snouts forced the heavy crates along the hard, earth-packed wharf, to the very edge, past the stern of the second ship.

Callie winced. The grunting of the boar and the scraping

of the crates must surely bring someone to investigate. She peered through the darkness.

All quiet.

More and more boxes and crates were moved into place.

By the broken fence, the whites of Peter's eyes shone in the dim moonlight, darting from the boar to the ships and back.

Callie shifted from leg to leg. 'Hurry, hurry,' she muttered.

The biggest sows were heaving against the last crate when a sailor came on deck. Callie stopped jiggling.

The sailor saw the crates and boxes all lined up. But not where they were supposed to be. He scratched his hair, then waved his arms.

'Boar! The boar are back!'

The sailor ran to the gangplank.

Madach rushed up from below.

The sailor didn't spot the chain. He fell to his face with a thump and a groan.

Callie skipped with delight, her hand on her mouth as several of his fellows, hard at his heels, tumbled on top of him.

It gave the boar more precious time.

Peter, watching the boar and not the Madach, cried out, 'Push! Push now!'

The boar pushed, their great heads and shoulders shoving at the heavy crates.

Splash, after splash, after splash!

Crates and boxes tumbled into the dark waters. Spumes of salt spray drenched the boar.

The Madach disentangled themselves from the chain and the chain from the railings and threw it aside – Jarrow would want to know later who the idiot person was who had tied it in the first place. They raced up the wharf to where the boar were heaving the last of the crates and boxes into the sea.

Many had bows and arrows, or carried long knives. Others waved sticks. Several carried lanterns to light the wharf.

All of them shouted.

'What are they doing?'

'The crates, look to the crates!'

'The engines, save the engines!'

Jarrow raged amid the chaos, bellowing orders which no one obeyed.

The boar charged back to Callie and Peter. The Madach with bows tried to take aim.

Callie couldn't breathe. Hurry, hurry!

The owls swooped on the archers, knocking the bows aside. Many of the Madach dropped their weapons and all of them waved their arms as the owls rose and dived, shrieking like ghouls, snapping at faces and eyes.

Foxes and badgers poured through the unbolted gate and the gap in the fence in a tangle of fur and claws. They slipped between the Madach's feet, tripping them up as the chain had done, biting and ripping at legs. The Madach shouted and jumped like bouncing balls to avoid the teeth and claws.

Callie gripped the fence post harder, barely daring to watch, fearful for her army. A Madach boot kicked a fox, sending it sprawling on the hard earth. Callie's heart stopped. The fox leaped to its feet and threw itself back into the battle.

The first boar reached the break in the fence and galloped into the Forest.

Peter called, 'Run, run, don't stop.' He glanced at Callie, frozen to her post on the other side of the gap. 'Callie, get out of here, quickly!'

Callie nodded and stayed where she was, waiting for the foxes and badgers to retreat through the gap too. The owls harried the flailing, shouting, kicking Madach, deflecting their aim, making swords and bows useless.

On the brightly lit wharf, Tristan cried out, 'The engines! Save the engines!' He flapped his arms in the faces of his fellow Madach, clumsily bumped into knife-wielding sailors and soldiers and stumbled into the archers. In his lurchings, he accidentally knocked aside lanterns, dousing their lights.

Callie grinned.

The last of the wild creatures raced through the fence.

Madach raced after them.

'Go, Callie, by the Beings get out of here!' Peter shouted.

Callie ran, stumbling as she reached the sudden dark of the trees. She twisted around to see where Peter was, and cried out.

He had tripped and fallen headlong to the ground.

Callie wheeled about. Peter scrambled to his feet, but the pursuing Madach were close now. A lantern shone on Peter's face. A soldier lunged for him.

A shrieking cry from the air rose above the shouts of the Madach and the grunts of the boar. Callie searched the dark sky.

Four cruelly taloned legs, the two front ones covered with feathers, bore down on the lunging soldier. The talons raked his back.

The soldier added his screams to Child's cries. He fell to the ground, writhing.

Callie's eyes widened as another soldier raised his bow, swiftly fitted an arrow and aimed it at Child.

'No!' Callie's scream was lost in the clamour.

The Madach let loose his arrow.

The strident cry came again. The eagle head lifted. Child's wings beat the air. He rose, away from the Madach, away from the arrows.

Crouched low on Child's back, a bump of darker brown against the lighter lion fur, Callie was certain she saw the rabbit. She closed her eyes, her heart thudding.

Go! Go!

Peter ran past her, grabbing at but missing Callie's arm. 'Run, run!'

Callie fled with the last of the foxes, weaving in and out of the trees and shrubs, losing herself in the forests of bracken.

The Madach gave chase, sprinting up the track to catch the young man they'd seen at the wharf.

And marvelling at the fantastical creature which had saved him.

***

In the village, the Danae listened to the distant shouting. What was happening?

Peter's father and mother knew their son was out in the Forest, beyond the imprisoning fence. They sat on the edge of their narrow bed and held each other's hands.

Meg, hunched in a chair in the tiny kitchen, stared into the smouldering ash of the fire. Her courage had fled once more.

Why hadn't she stopped Callie? Why?

Chapter Thirty Five

Captain Jarrow's Fury

The master engineer paced up and down Captain Jarrow's cabin. His eyes were hollow and red-rimmed. He'd had no sleep, had toiled all night on the wharf collecting those bits of machinery which had fallen from the open crates and trying, without success, to think of a way to bring any closed crates up from the sea-bed.

Yes, he explained to Captain Jarrow, chewing on his lip, there were no spare parts for the spare parts, and yes, most of the important pieces of the machines had been washed out with the tides to become playgrounds for fish. A few bits remained, laid out beneath the canvas shelters, and one or two boxes.

The machines would not be built.

Captain Jarrow clenched his jaw. 'I want that Danae, I want his head. And anybody else who was there!' The whole ship heard him. 'And how, by all the Beings, did he train those damn animals to do what they did? And what was that … that … monster?'

The Madach who had been attacked by Child lay on his front in his berth, his back covered in salves and bandages, his ruined shirt a bloodied tangle on the floor.

Tristan tried to stay out of the way, hugging his joy to himself. If anyone caught his eye, he would knit his brows, shake his head and shrug dejectedly, clearly devastated at this setback to Lord Rafe's plans.

Captain Jarrow went to Tomas, who had watched the raid through the porthole of his cabin and was rejoicing too, not as secretly as Tristan.

'I have a task for you today, Master Tomas.' Captain Jarrow's snarl was met with blankness. 'You're coming with me to the village. If we don't find that rebel Danae there, you'll make sure your people understand their punishment for this destruction will be swift and fierce.'

He glowered at Tomas, who glowered back.

Captain Jarrow had the last word. 'I want that vandal on this ship, locked up.'

***

In the early morning, as the mists rose from the Forest outside the tall fence, Madach soldiers with swords and knives and sailors with sticks, marched into the village. They threw open front doors, ordered villagers to leave their breakfasts and hurry to the square, at once. They climbed steps to sleeping rooms and steered sleepy and half-dressed villagers out of their cottages and along the winding paths between the white houses to the square.

Those already gathered at the gate to leave the village for their work were told to stay where they were, the request underlined by more Madach waving more swords.

The anxious Danae gathered in small groups, eyeing the Madach weapons, whispering to each other. Mothers fussed around unusually docile children, keeping them close. People who had had no time to throw on shawls and coats against the dawn chill, hugged themselves and stamped their feet.

Matthew, the blacksmith, stood apart, arms folded, until a muscular Madach soldier pushed him at knifepoint into the crowded square. Matthew's wife, her baby in her arms, clung to his side. Elder Judith comforted her.

Captain Jarrow paced up and down, lips pursed, pale eyes

176

bulging. His face shone red with fury.

No one, Madach or Danae, dared approach him.

With a soldier either side of him, Tomas stood at the edge of the square. His hands were bound in front of him. His head was down. The villagers eyed their senior Elder, frowning at how haggard and pale he was. And cowed. Not the defiant Tomas they knew. The soldiers rebuffed any Danae who tried to approach.

Meg was there, hardly able to stand, shivering and white. Something brushed her hand, making her jump. Sensing Meg's legs starting to buckle, Callie put her arm around Meg's waist.

An angry bile rose in Callie's throat at the confused faces of the Danae, some in their nightwear with shawls and coats thrown over their shoulders, some wearing shoes with no socks on their feet.

'The girl with the ball!' Captain Jarrow pointed at the guard who had let Suzie out of the gate. 'Which one is she?'

The guard paced among the Danae, scowling at every little girl. It wasn't long before he found Suzie.

'This one.'

Callie felt ill. What would they do to her friend? She started to step to the front to tell this awful Captain Jarrow it was her they wanted, not Suzie.

Meg gripped her arm. 'Wait.'

Suzie's mother stood behind her daughter.

Captain Jarrow bore down on them like a rampaging bear.

He snarled into Suzie's white face. 'I'm tempted to have you hauled to the ship, locked up and the key thrown into the sea.'

The Danae gasped.

'No!' Suzie's mother pulled her daughter close. 'What has she done?'

'Do you want to go too?'

'If necessary.' Suzie's mother narrowed her eyes at Captain Jarrow.

The Danae buzzed, a swarm of angry bees. They wouldn't

stand for this. How dare Jarrow threaten little girls and their mothers?

Elder Judith pushed her way forward to plant herself between Captain Jarrow and Suzie's mother.

'Captain Jarrow,' she said, calmly. 'Whatever has happened, surely you cannot believe this child had anything to do with it?'

Jarrow ignored her. He appeared to forget Suzie, instead glaring at the buzzing Danae.

'Where's this fellow who led the attack?'

Relief washed through Callie. Peter was alive, and free.

The Danae sneaked sly looks at each other.

What attack?

Had someone struck a blow against their captors? Something bad enough to bring this fury from Captain Jarrow? A few exchanged tiny smirks with their neighbours.

Captain Jarrow bellowed across the square. 'We know what you look like!'

Elder Judith tried again. 'What's going on?'

Jarrow shoved her aside to stride in among the muttering villagers.

'All the men, over there.' He waved his hand at one side of the square.

No one budged.

Captain Jarrow glared around. He beckoned to the Madach, who took several steps closer to the villagers, hands on the hilts of knives and swords, sticks tapping against their legs.

First one, then another, and finally all the Danae men walked with slow, reluctant steps to the side of the square. Even Matthew. The Madach sailors and soldiers who had been on the wharf the night before went from one man to the next, ignoring the older ones, taking careful stock of the younger men.

'Not here,' they said.

Captain Jarrow scowled at the villagers. 'Listen well, you Danae. Your senior Elder's got something to say to you all.'

He pushed Tomas forward.

The silence in the square was absolute.

Tomas lifted his bound hands.

'Danae, as you can see, I am a prisoner of these Madach, although I have committed no crime. If I escape back to you, they threaten they will set fire to this village and make us all live in the ruins, like wild dogs.'

A low moan of shock cracked the silence.

'If the person who led the attack last night is not delivered to Captain Jarrow by this evening, I'm told we will suffer this fate in any case. I'm sorry.' Tomas' head went down.

'We don't know who it was,' the inn-keeper said. 'We don't know anything about it, whatever it is that's happened.'

Captain Jarrow snorted. 'I suggest you find out, and soon. You must know who's missing. And you'd better find him.'

Through the crowd, Callie saw Peter's mother and father huddle closer together.

Amid the angry and frightened mumblings of the Danae, Jarrow stamped from the square and out through the gate. Tomas was shoved along behind him.

Callie followed Tomas and his guard, muttering *You can't see me*, as she slunk through the gate. She was about to run into the trees when she heard Captain Jarrow speaking to the guards.

'I want every house and shed searched, although I don't expect to find him here. I'd wager he's in the forest with those pigs. Good company for each other!'

No one laughed.

'I want more guards on this fence,' Jarrow said, 'and no more outside working parties. These people can go without bread and their crops can rot in the ground. We'll take the livestock for ourselves, at least until we're ready to leave this place. Understood?'

'Yes, sir.'

'Yes, Captain.'

'At once, sir.'

'And I want that flying beast caught. Alive! If it's what I think it is, it's worth as much as all these trouble-making Danae put together.'

Callie crossed the track and ran through the Forest to the willow tree.

***

Madach soldiers with unsheathed swords held the fearful Danae in the square while sailors and woodsmen searched houses and sheds, climbing the narrow stairs to peer under beds, poking their noses into pigsties and chicken coops.

Suzie's mother hugged her daughter. 'What happened? What did you do?'

Suzie didn't know what she'd done.

'It's all right Ma, it's all right,' she said.

She supposed she should be angry at Callie for putting her in danger. She wasn't. She felt proud, like a heroine from one of the old fairytales.

***

Meg realised Callie was no longer at her side. She'd slipped away, gone through the gate with the Madach, invisible to them as usual.

Her anxiety, already high with the morning's events, grew. What was the girl up to? How would she get back in? What would Jarrow do if he caught her? Meg wrapped her arms about herself and eyed the sword-bearing guards as she would wolves about to strike.

Chapter Thirty Six

Peter's Fate

After the attack, Callie had fled first to the willow and afterwards searched for Peter before stealing back to the village. There she found Madach posted all around the fence, their lanterns swinging as they scanned between the trees. She'd shrunk back into the Forest and waited, not sleeping, watching the gate.

In the early morning, cold and stiff, she'd crept into the village behind the furious Jarrow and his soldiers and sailors and hidden beside the inn to see what would happen. From there, she'd seen Meg, with Jethro's family and the other villagers, shepherded into the square. Now she had escaped again, wanting to find Peter.

Callie leaned against the willow's trunk, catching her breath. She waited.

Sure enough, the rabbit soon arrived, skipping and jumping and waggling its long ears.

'Thank the Beings you're safe.' Callie picked up the rabbit and stroked its quivering nose. 'Whatever were you doing?'

Someone had to fetch Child. It's his Forest, after all.

The Guardian. The new Guardian. Yes, it made sense.

Callie placed the rabbit on the ground. 'Thank goodness neither of you are hurt, and it was brave, saving Peter. But the Madach saw Peter's face. They want him.'

The rabbit waggled its ears. *Let them try and find him!*

'That's the problem.' Callie grimaced. 'If he isn't found, evil

Captain Jarrow will burn the village and make us live in the ruins. He's furious.'

The rabbit's ears went down.

'Do you know where Peter is? Can you take me to him?'

The rabbit rose on its back legs, sniffed the air, and hopped onto a thin trail which led deeper into the Forest.

It wasn't long before the rabbit left the trail and led Callie in among the trees and bushes. She had to scramble through bracken and try her best to avoid nettles while keeping the rabbit's white tail in sight. The day had warmed and Callie's tongue stuck to the inside of her parched mouth. She wished she'd drunk from the stream by the willow when she'd had the chance.

At last the rabbit stopped in a small clearing bright with pink foxgloves and ringed with thick-leaved beeches. Callie pushed back her sweaty hair, straining to see between the trees into the darker Forest beyond.

'Peter, are you here?'

Peter stepped out from the other side of the clearing. His yellow hair was mussed and leaves and twigs stuck to his shirt, jerkin and trousers.

'Callie! You're safe! What's happening? Did it work? Are the Madach angry? Are they looking for me? Did you get back home?'

'Yes, to all those questions. Although angry isn't the right word. Jarrow is furious. He's threatening to make us pay a high price for this.'

Callie sat on a tree stump and plucked at a pocket of moss. 'He says if you're not found and given over to him, he'll ... he'll burn the village. Make us live in the ruins, like wild dogs.'

Peter sank to the ground, arms clasped about his legs. He put his head on his knees.

Callie watched him. A bird called. Otherwise, the Forest was listless in the late morning heat.

Peter lifted his head. 'I can't let them burn the village, can I? Burning the village is too terrible a price.'

Callie picked at threads of moss. Peter must make the decision himself.

'What do you think Jarrow will do to me, if I go back?'

'Lock you up, like Tomas.' Callie thought of Tomas, haggard and unkempt. She shivered despite her sweating back.

'Even so, I have to go home.' Peter pulled himself to his feet. 'I never was fond of camping in the woods, anyway.' He grinned a sickly grin.

'I'm sorry,' Callie said. 'I knew I had to tell you.'

'Yes, you did, and I'm sorry they saw me and glad they didn't see you.' He squinted at Callie. 'Although why .... oh, never mind.' He flipped a strand of hair out of his eyes. 'And what was that ... thing ... which attacked the Madach?'

'Child. They tried to shoot him.'

'Child? Not like any child I know. From the glimpse I had, it was more like a monstrous eagle with a lion's tail.' He frowned. 'You've seen it before?'

'Yes,' Callie said. 'He's a gryphon and he lives in a cave on the other side of the ridge, except the cave's not always there.'

Peter's eyebrows rose.

'It's too hard to explain,' Callie said. 'He's only a baby though, and he's our friend. And Jarrow wants him captured, to sell, like he plans to sell us.'

Callie wanted to cry.

'It's all right.' Peter placed his hand on Callie's back. 'We've struck a massive blow which will really hurt these Madach. We should be proud. Your wild army too.' He smiled at the rabbit. 'But we'd better get back before Jarrow starts lighting fires.'

The rabbit hopped to the edge of the clearing and Peter followed. When Callie stayed where she was, Peter stopped. 'Come on. Your ma'll be desperate.'

'No. I'm not going back.'

'What?'

'Jarrow's not going to let anybody out again. No more work parties.'

'Lock us up properly? What about the farmers, the mill ...?'

'Exactly.' Callie pulled at an untidy curl. 'I don't want to be stuck inside any fence. And I have to make sure Child isn't caught.' She looked at the rabbit. 'My friends will take care of me.'

'What about your ma? Can you do this to her?'

Callie, her eyes damp, sighed. 'I have to. Try to tell her I'll be all right, if you get the chance. Tell her, have courage. She'll understand.'

Peter still hesitated. 'I'm not sure she will. In fact, I'm pretty sure she won't like it at all.'

'Remind her what I told her about Tristan, about my good Madach. Make sure she knows it's a secret. Tell her he'll look after me. I'll be fine, truly.'

'If I get the chance.' Peter gave Callie a sideways look. 'Tristan. Sorry about before, doubting him. He was great, wasn't he?'

'Yes.' Callie nodded hard. 'The rabbit was right.'

The rabbit preened one long ear.

Peter sucked in a huge breath. 'Okay, rabbit, let's go.'

The rabbit headed once more for the edge of the clearing.

'Good luck.' Peter waved.

'Good luck to you, too.' Callie waved back.

***

Peter presented himself to the Madach guards. He straightened his shoulders. 'It's me you want.'

Not far inside the gate, which was open to let the Madach searchers through, Peter saw Meg staring out. Her lips were clamped together, her forehead creased.

He called to her. 'Meg, everything's fine, don't worry! You must have courage!'

Meg briefly closed her eyes, nodded. Her mouth relaxed into the faintest smile.

'No talking!' A guard dealt Peter a blow to the head which nearly sent him to the ground.

'Leave him be!' Meg rushed at the guard, beating at his chest with her fists. 'Bullies! Cowards!'

He shoved her roughly back inside.

The gate banged closed. The bolt was thrown into place with an echoing clang.

A soldier tied Peter's hands and dragged him over the ridge and down through the trees. It was a very short time before they came to the ships, and the waiting Captain Jarrow.

Peter held himself upright. Captain Jarrow's bushy ginger beard nevertheless loomed above Peter's head.

'So you're the vandal who destroyed Lord Rafe's machines, hey?' Captain Jarrow's voice was thick with anger. 'What should I do to you, hey?'

Peter stared at a stain on Captain Jarrow's grubby waistcoat.

Captain Jarrow thrust his beard into Peter's face. 'Throwing you to the sharks would be too good for you.'

Peter blanched. His leg shook.

Captain Jarrow flicked his wrist. 'Take him away.' He gestured at the soldiers. 'Lock him up with his senior Elder. They can spend their time feeling sorry for each other.'

The guard hustled the relieved Peter out of the cabin.

Behind him, Peter heard Captain Jarrow snigger.

'And they'll both pay in the end, in the slave markets.'

Chapter Thirty Seven

'Be proud'

Roughened bedclothes, emptied drawers, overturned barrels and spilled baskets of fruit and vegetables marked the Madach's search of the village.

Although not long past midday, most people had crammed into the stuffy inn to talk over the morning's events in hushed tones. Quiet children played under the tables.

No one noticed Meg come in and walk quickly to where the miller and his wife sat on a settle by the cold fireplace. She squatted beside them and spoke, her face animated, hands gesturing.

They listened, nodding. The miller's wife produced a wobbly smile.

With the help of the miller, Meg jumped up onto the settle.

'Danae,' she called.

The room quietened, each table of villagers whispering to the next to hush and listen.

'Danae.' Meg's voice was strong and urgent. 'I have something to tell you all.' She looked around at the curious faces. Her voice rose. 'We should be proud today, not cowed by Jarrow and his bully guards and soldiers. Last night we struck a solid blow against these invaders.'

She stepped down from the settle, put her arms around the waists of the miller and his wife.

'Last night, Peter and my Callie destroyed the Madach's

machines, monstrous machines which would have cut through our Forest, destroying our home.'

'More about those fantasy machines, Meg? A child's imaginings?' Elder James' disdainful voice broke the puzzled silence which followed Meg's speech.

'Not imaginings, James,' Meg said. 'I believe my child, although it may be too late. Whatever happened, Jarrow's temper tells us he's suffered a mighty blow to his plans for our Forest.'

'And at what price, Meg?' the Elder said. 'Peter locked up, Callie – a child – hiding in the Forest, and the rest of us captive in our homes, unable to work our farms or see to our cattle. What price?'

His caterpillar eyebrows knitted across his forehead. He spread out his arms, appealing against such foolish behaviour. Other Elders, seated with him at a long table, solemnly nodded their agreement.

'Humph!' The miller paced across the room. He placed his hands flat on the table in front of Elder James and glared.

'You Elders should be ashamed,' he said, 'that children have had to show us how to stop these Madach before they destroy the whole Forest.'

He turned from the Elders, walked back to Meg, grabbed her hand and raised it high. 'Let's be proud!' he called.

Matthew rose from his seat. 'Let's be proud!'

The villagers didn't understand what all this was about. But they were moved by Meg's emotion and cheered by the miller's spirit.

'Let's be proud!' they called to each other.

They banged the tables with their mugs and fists, grinning.

Outside the fence, a Madach guard heard the cheers and the banging. He wondered what the captive Danae had to be happy about.

**

Callie rested her back against a beech, her legs outstretched. She was so tired.

She was also frightened. They had slowed Lord Rafe's destruction, but in return they'd made things much worse for the Danae. And for Peter, and for Child. She should go to Child. Callie yawned. She was too weary to make her way to the ridge and would she find the grassy bowl by herself?

Callie's heart grew heavy, overcome by a deep loneliness. She wished none of this had ever happened. She wished Lucy, Mark and Gwen, and Da, were all here, with her, in the Forest, with no Madach to worry about.

The deep dread rose, the nightmares spinning through her head, vivid even in the hot, sunny clearing.

... the animals flee, their fear sears her mind ...

This time, there was no hissing monster.

Callie thought of Peter braving his fears about Tristan to go ahead with the attack, and now braving Captain Jarrow and certain imprisonment. And she thought of Tristan too, doing what he believed was the right thing instead of what others expected him to do.

Between them, and with the Forest creatures, they had killed the hissing monster. Peter was right, they should be proud.

Yet Callie could still see the Danae, thin and hungry, hands bound. And in her tired mind the market sellers still called, '*A fairytale come to life, my lords and ladies!*'

A fairytale. Sold as fairytale slaves. What could they do to steer aside such a fate? Had Gwen and Mark found the Sleih? Had they been able to persuade the Sleih to rescue the villagers?

Callie sighed deeply. Her heavy eyelids closed against the shards of sunlight winking between the leaves.

She was falling into sleep when she heard a soft thud. Her eyes flew open. A blue-feathered head brushed at Callie's hair. A long sinewy tail with a fluffy white bob curved around to tickle her face.

'Child!' Callie stroked the feathered neck as Child stretched his tawny body beside her and rested his head in her lap. His green eyes looked into Callie's own green-eyed gaze.

They fell asleep, curled together between the roots of the beech.

In Callie's dreams, golden-crowned kings and queens on fine, long-legged horses swept along the ridge and down through the Forest to the Madach ships. They brandished gleaming swords and chased the cowering Madach into the sea.

Chapter Thirty Eight

The Seer

Lady Melda of the House of Alder and Seer of the people Sleih, held the reins of her tall black horse loosely in her hands. The horse's prettily painted hooves danced lightly on the stony track as if about to take flight.

A cool wind belied the fact it was summer. Through light veils of rain, Lady Melda stared past the cottages and farmhouses dotted along the sides of the green valley below, to an elegant although small castle standing at the valley's head. Pulling her cloak about her, Lady Melda picked out the castle's highest tower.

She had reached her destination.

It was the rat which had told her the story. The rat had learned it from the foxes who'd been sent to ask other creatures to help the Danae children travelling through the Forest. They were full of the importance of their errand and the tales of what was happening in the Forest. The rat considered this was a story of possible interest to Lady Melda, and in this it was correct. She'd immediately seen the possibilities. First, however, she had to discover where these invading Madach came from, who had sent them and what this person's plans might be for the Forest – and beyond.

Lady Melda had spent many weeks locked in her solar high above the Citadel of Ilatias, casting her mind this way and that, seeking and probing. She had finally found Lord Rafe on his tower, marvelling at his own victories and wondering, as he often did, how his northern expedition was faring.

Her journey from the Citadel had been long and arduous, despite the tall black horse's speed and lightness of foot. She had first ridden a short way west from the Citadel, crossing to the southern lands where the strait between north and south was at its narrowest and dotted with islands.

The island ferrymen had been curious about this grand lady travelling on her own, without even a servant. Afterwards, however, when their wives wanted to know if there'd been any interesting passengers today, they'd shaken their heads, no, no one interesting. Simply the normal traders and farmers.

Lady Melda had ridden far east, passing through Lord Rafe's conquered lands to reach Etting itself. What she'd seen of the conquered lands impressed her. This Lord Rafe was a man who understood how to get the most out of his people.

Now she was here, soon to meet Lord Rafe face to face.

Lady Melda was quite sure Lord Rafe would be willing to be drawn into her plans. If not of his own volition, then certainly of hers.

***

Lord Rafe was in his study. Spread in front of him across the great oak table was the map from Captain Jarrow's chart room, the one he'd shown Tristan before the northern expedition left on its voyage.

He gazed at the map without seeing it, asking himself, for the hundredth time, what was happening. Were the holds filled with timbers and whatever other bounty had been found? Were they preparing to return, heading home before the winter storms?

He ached to know.

Of course, the ships could be at the bottom of the ocean or lost to pirates. Lord Rafe refused to consider this possibility, because if the ships were lost, all would have been for nothing.

Failure was not to be countenanced.

It occurred to him it would also mean Tristan was lost. Lord Rafe knew he should feel sorrier than he did about this. He stroked his beard, recalling Tristan's foolish attitudes. Pitying the conquered peoples! The memory made him drop into his chair. He stretched out his booted legs and closed his eyes. An exasperated sigh ruffled the papers on the desk. Whether Tristan was alive or not, Lord Rafe did need to think about re-marrying, get himself a more worthy heir, or two.

The room grew dark. Lord Rafe was about to call for a servant to light the lamps and build up the fire, when his head steward knocked and entered.

'My lord, you have a visitor who declares she has travelled a long distance to gain audience with you. She claims to be a Lady of the Sleih.'

'The Sleih?' Lord Rafe scoffed. 'Fairytales and folk lore, there's no such thing as Sleih.'

'My lord, this lady does not appear to be a Madach. She claims to have travelled from the north, from a place called the Citadel of Ilatias. She declares she has business which will benefit you.'

'Does she indeed? The north, eh? Well, Sleih or not, shouldn't keep a lady waiting I suppose. Take her to the Green Room and bring us wine and food.'

The steward withdrew and Lord Rafe prepared to follow.

Before doing so, he took a moment to glance at the map, where the northern lands were marked 'Uninhabited (?)'.

Obviously not, if this lady was telling the truth. She might know something of his expedition.

Chapter Thirty Nine

Power And Riches

Rafe's visitor was standing by the fire when he came in to meet her.

The cloak she was removing – a deep blue garment trimmed with silver fur – suggested wealth. Rafe thought her clothes didn't bear much evidence of long, hard travelling. Her blue dress fell un-muddied and unwrinkled to the floor. Its long sleeves and neckline were edged with fine silver embroidery, untarnished and sparkling. Her dark hair was neatly braided high on top of her head. Blue sapphires and diamonds set in silver were tucked into the braids, their glitter competing with the brightness of the fire. Her skin, the colour of pale honey, was unmarred by signs of weary travel.

The lady herself was slim and not very tall, coming perhaps to Rafe's chest. Nevertheless, she carried her short height with a haughty assurance.

The lady turned to Rafe. He was immediately drawn to her eyes. They were the colour of the green northern oceans and a little too large for her delicate face. For some reason, Rafe grew a little dizzy, unable to look away. The lady briefly held his eyes before directing her gaze back to the fire. Rafe shook his head, the dizziness gone.

'My lady, my steward tells me you are a Lady of the Sleih who has travelled from the far north to see me.'

She bent her head.

'If such is indeed the case,' Rafe said, 'I am truly flattered, and would know what business brings you here. First, however, I would know your name and station, if I may?'

The lady took a step nearer to Rafe.

'I am Lady Melda of the House of Alder of the people Sleih. Among my people I am a Seer, one who is wise in the ways of the Sleih and with certain powers at my disposal.'

Rafe was inclined to believe her. His dizziness when first she looked at him had been unsettling. He grew wary, then laughed at himself. He, Rafe, wary of a small woman!

'You are wise to be wary, Lord Rafe,' the lady said, bringing Rafe's head up sharply.

The lady seated herself in a cushioned chair by a low table near the fire. 'But if you will hear me out,' she said, 'I have much to say which will be of interest to you. I believe we seek similar ends. I believe our paths should be joined to achieve these, to our great mutual benefit.'

A servant came into the room and laid wine and food on the table. Rafe dismissed the servant, indicating they would serve themselves. He poured two drinks and handed a glass to the lady, holding his own up to hers in a welcome gesture.

'My Lady Melda, I am anxious to hear what you have to say,' Rafe said, sitting the other side of the fire. 'Also, what you know of my ambitions. If, as you say, we can help each other, I would be most willing to talk further.'

Rafe was surprised at his own words. He had no idea who this woman really was. As his steward said, however, the lady did not appear to be Madach and there was definitely a sense of power about her. It would do Rafe no harm to hear what she had to say.

And, she was a beautiful woman. Hadn't he only now been thinking of re-marrying?

The lady coughed softly.

'What I know of your ambitions, my Lord Rafe, is this,'

she said. 'You have had success in expanding your Duchy of Etting, conquering lands immediately to the south, west and east of here. From your tower, all you view is yours. Well done,' she said.

Normally, Rafe would have taken exception to her condescending tone. Instead he said, 'Go on,' while asking himself how she knew about the tower.

'I also know you have sent an expedition north, across the oceans.'

'What do you know of my expedition?' Rafe leaned forward eagerly. 'Have you seen it? Has it landed?'

'It has landed. And it has discovered more than trees on the shores of the northern lands.'

'Excellent, excellent,' Rafe said. 'What more than trees? Do you know?'

Piles of gold and silver, heaps of rubies and diamonds flitted through his dreaming mind.

'Danae,' the lady said. 'Your expedition has discovered the Danae of The Forest.'

Rafe narrowed his eyes. First Sleih, now Danae. Was the lady mocking him?

'I believe you know of what I speak,' the lady said, 'and therefore you will know there are many Madach lords and ladies who would pay much to have a Danae in their service. For the pure novelty of it. Imagine! A fairytale come to life! Such a delight, such a way of making the neighbours jealous. Such cute playthings for the children.'

It might not be gold and rubies, which was a disappointment. But Rafe could see the value. If it was true.

'Moreover, it appears there are not many of these Danae. Their rarity will much increase the prices you could command.'

Ah! Rafe forgot about trees and gold and pondered Danae. An idea occurred to him. If these Danae existed, what about the Sleih this woman said she was from? Was there more value there?

'In the northern lands – which are inhabited – the Sleih are not considered a fairytale, Lord Rafe. Moreover, those who know us would not dare consider imprisoning us, or taking us as servants.'

Rafe stared at her. How did she know what he was thinking?

The lady went on. 'I also know this. Two children of the Danae are on their way to the Citadel to ask the Sleih for help defending their Forest from your expedition. If they are successful, you will not have your trees and you will not have your Danae.'

The lady held her glass to her lips and watched Rafe over the rim.

Rafe took a sip of wine, closed his eyes for a moment and spoke. 'You are saying I am within reach of a valuable cargo, or two, counting the forest itself. However, there is a danger I may not get either as the Sleih – your people by what you have said – may snatch both from me.'

'Correct.'

Rafe tried to stare directly at the lady. He grew dizzy. He faced the fire.

'If you are of the Sleih, why are you here to warn me of this? I assume it's to do with the mutual benefit you referred to earlier. Perhaps you could enlighten me?'

'Surely,' she said. The lady also looked into the fire. It flared, seeming to set alight the mirrored walls.

'I have said I am a Seer of the people Sleih. As such, I am held in respect and have much influence with the king. However, the king is soft and the Sleih grow soft with him, living in luxury with little to challenge them. They choose not to take advantage of the powers which we Seers could bring to the kingdom.'

She shifted to face Rafe, who, considering it unwise to look into those eyes, remained looking at the fire.

'To be open with you, my Lord Rafe, my ambition is to rule the Citadel of Ilatias and the lands surrounding it.' She paused and Rafe nodded as if this was a perfectly normal ambition.

'This is how I see it,' the lady said. 'If these children reach the Citadel, I can ensure their pleas are not granted and they must make their way back to their Forest empty-handed. In return, I seek your help, when the time comes, in taking the Citadel and appointing myself its new ruler. I would pay homage to Etting, of course, as do the lands you have already conquered. The Citadel itself is quite a prize. Your coffers would be well-filled from its riches. It will become even wealthier, under the right rule.' She bowed her head. 'What say you, my lord? Do you appreciate the mutual benefits I propose?'

Rafe considered. A short time ago, he'd been worrying about whether the northern expedition had reached its destination. Now he was being offered not merely the bounty he sought, but in addition one of possibly equal value, plus this place called the Citadel.

He reached back into memory, searching for what he knew about the fabled Sleih. He remembered their home was said to be a magnificent city, the streets paved with gold and windows made of diamonds. There were gold and diamonds to be had after all.

He raised his glass again to the lady, trying once more to gaze directly into her eyes. This time, by looking quickly away, he was able to do so without the dizziness.

'My lady, I foresee a mutually beneficial partnership. Let me arrange for you to rest awhile before we meet over dinner, when we can discuss how we might take our plans further.'

'Thank you, my lord.'

Rafe called for his steward. As the lady was led out, Rafe could hear her question the steward about the stabling of her horse. The door closed after them.

Alone, Rafe pondered how he'd come to trust this strange

woman so quickly and so fully. It all made sense, he told himself. They each got something. As it should be.

He sipped the remains of his wine, visions of limitless riches dancing in the yellow flames of the fire.

End of Book One

If you have enjoyed this book, please leave a review on Amazon.com or Amazon.co.uk.

Quests

Chapter One

A Boar And A Bear

Boom!

The thunderous shock drowned out for a heartbeat the shrieking of the wind. Mark jumped. He drew his cloak tighter about his shivering body. A vision of far away home brought self-pitying tears to his already wet eyes.

'We have to get out of this!'

'Where?' Gwen's voice sounded thin, pitched against the hammering rain. 'I can't see anything, it's too dark.'

Lightning lit the gnarled trees.

Mark jolted backwards.

What was that?

Gwen screamed. She clutched Mark's arm.

'A bear! It's a bear! Run!'

Another flash lit the trees. A monstrous black shape reared

above Mark. Its roar matched the thunder.

Mark's throat went dry. He jerked the arm Gwen grasped. 'Run, Gwen, run!'

The dark came down, darker than before the lightning.

Something heavy and moving fast brushed past Mark.

More bears? His terror grew.

Whatever it was butted him hard. He grabbed at Gwen, pulling her with him, into the mud.

An unearthly squealing added to Gwen's screams and to the crash of the thunder and the roaring of the bear.

Mark spluttered, trying to stand, to run. Gwen floundered beside him.

The squealing went on, and on, pitched high against the deep bellow of the bear.

Mark lurched to his feet.

Lightning, a short flash, enough for Mark to glimpse the biggest boar he'd ever seen. The creature struggled with the bear, long tusks impaled in the dark fur, its hind legs thrust into the muddy earth. The bear howled, twisting its body to shake the boar free.

Darkness.

The uproar from the bear and the boar challenged the boom of thunder and the screech of the wind.

Mark tugged at Gwen's cloak. 'Come on!'

They clung to each other, stumbling through the slippery wetness. Thin branches slapped at Mark's face and tore at his clothes. Stones and roots grabbed his feet.

Shelter. They needed shelter.

Mark squinted through the rain. His breath came in spasms. His cloak wrapped its sodden wetness around his legs. Any moment, he would fall where he was.

'There!' He pointed to a darker gap between the trees. 'It might be a cave.'

Gwen ran towards the darkness, squelching through unseen

puddles. Mark splashed beside her. Water seeped through his cracked boots, soaking his chilled feet. Flashes of lightning lit their way.

Gwen stopped in front of an ivy covered gash in the rock. 'Might be more bears.' She shivered. 'Or wolves.'

Mark gulped deep breaths. They had to get out of the storm. He pushed through the ivy to lean into the cave. No smell of wild animals. He poked a leg through the gap, listening. Nothing, except his own heart thudding in his ears.

'It's safe.'

Gwen fell through the ivy behind him, into the dryness and quiet. And the pitch blackness. Mark heard the soft thump as Gwen slumped to the hard ground. He dropped beside her, his wet cloak bunched at his back. He could smell the dankness of mud and last year's leaves on his hair and clothes.

Gwen let out a shuddering sigh. 'What ... happened?'

'A boar ... a boar, huge! It pushed me over.'

'It saved us ... didn't it? From ... the bear.'

'Saved us? You think it meant to save us?' Mark found the idea startling.

'No.' Gwen noisily sucked in air. 'It wanted the bear. We were in its way.' She let out a deep breath. 'I suppose.'

Beyond the curtain of ivy, the clatter of the rain had quietened and the thunder and lightning had moved on through the Deep Forest. The wind's squalling turned fitful, as if it too was tired of the storm and wanted to rest.

'Listen,' Gwen said.

'What?'

'There's a noise, not the wind, something else. Do you hear it?'

Mark strained to hear. There it was, above the faltering wind. A wild howl, answered by another, and another.

'Wolves,' Gwen said. 'Again.'

The cries of wolves had followed them for many days, the

202

fearsome noise seeming closer each night. Every evening, Mark made sure the fire blazed hotly bright, waking from time to time to keep the flames glowing. He and Gwen slept close together, as near to the blaze as they dared.

'It's too dark to see if there's anything to light a fire with,' Mark said.

The howling stopped.

'Let's hope the wolves stay at home tonight, out of this storm.'

Mark heard the tiredness in his sister's voice. He shivered and rubbed his hands together. 'Isn't it summer? Isn't it supposed to be warm? And not rain as much?' He wanted to distract them both from frightening visions of wolves and bears. And wild boar big enough to attack bears.

'We have storms like this at home in the summer, too, remember?'

'Home.' Mark sighed. 'It's been forever since we left home.'

'Yes. And still no clue if we're getting closer to these Sleih. It's all well and good to say the Sleih are in the west, if anyone knew how far west.'

'Assuming there are Sleih.'

It was a conversation he and Gwen had every day while they traipsed along the flattened grass of animal trails which more often than not ended at a prickly holly or a stand of nettles or a stony cliff edge. Trying to keep west, they'd splashed across countless streams, slipped and slithered on mossy stones, scrambled up steep banks and pushed their way through scrub-filled valleys.

The forest itself seemed to not want to help. It wasn't like their own friendly Forest with playful streams and trees which stayed in the same place year in and year out. The deeper they wandered into this forest, the deeper the darkness below the ancient trees, the fewer trails there were – and the more of them which led nowhere – and the stranger the night grunts and whistles and whispers which disturbed their unquiet rest. They'd camped beside tall leafy beech trees to wake the next morning under a willow, or an ash tree. Had the trees moved? Had they themselves been moved?

Mark had seen Gwen's strained, unbelieving face and known his own was the same. The creeping chill of feeling constantly watched never left him.

Then the wolves started their nightly howling. And now there were bears and giant boar to worry about.

And they still didn't know if there were any Sleih to be found.

'I don't think we'll ever reach these Sleih,' Mark said, as he did every day. 'I think they're a fairytale. And if they are real, and if we find them, why would they want to help us?'

Mark heard Gwen shifting on the dry floor.

'I don't know,' she said. 'I only know we promised Ma we'd bring back an army of Sleih and we have to keep on until we either reach the Sleih or find out they don't exist.'

'And Lucy, too,' Mark said. 'We've got to try and find Lucy.'

In the dark cave, wet and cold, the task was overwhelming. He lay down, wriggling to find a spot where a stone didn't jab into him, pushing a damp bag into place to serve as a pillow. 'What I wouldn't give to hear Ma yelling at me to hurry up with the firewood before the stove went out.'

'I know.' Gwen sighed. 'And Callie carrying on about the animals.' She paused. 'Callie, the animals ...'

'What about Callie and her animals?'

'Nothing, not really. It's what she said about the wild creatures helping us. Why would she say that?'

Mark grunted. Callie was strange, that was all he knew.

The sound of Gwen pummelling her own pillow-bag reached him. 'Let's try and sleep, see what the morning brings.'

***

Go to my website cherylburman.com to find out what inspired *The Guardians Of The Forest*. You can also buy Book Two *Quests* and Book Three *Gryphon Magic* from there or direct from Amazon.com or Amazon.co.uk in both kindle and paperback versions.

Printed in Great Britain
by Amazon